"ADAMS! TURN AROUND!"

Clint turned and saw that he was facing three men. He waited to see which one was the spokesman. That was usually the man he'd have to kill first.

"You *are* Clint Adams, aren't you?" the man in the center asked.

"That's right."

"I guess you know what we're here for."

"Well," Clint said, "if you're no different from every other damn fool I seem to run across, yeah, I know why you're here. Damn fools are the only ones I know who want to die before breakfast."

Clint looked at the man in the middle.

"You going to let me put aside my saddlebags and rifle?" he asked.

"What for?" the man asked. "Your gun hand is free."

And he went for his gun. . . .

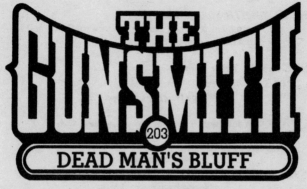

THE GUNSMITH

203

DEAD MAN'S BLUFF

J. R. ROBERTS

J

JOVE BOOKS, NEW YORK

DEAD MAN'S BLUFF

A Jove Book / published by arrangement with
the author

PRINTING HISTORY
Jove edition / December 1998

The Penguin Putnam Inc. World Wide Web site address is
http://www.penguinputnam.com

ISBN: 0-515-12414-1

A JOVE BOOK®
Jove Books are published by The Berkley Publishing Group,
a member of Penguin Putnam Inc.,
375 Hudson Street, New York, New York 10014.
JOVE and the "J" design are trademarks
belonging to Jove Publications, Inc.

PRINTED IN THE UNITED STATES OF AMERICA

10 9 8 7 6 5 4 3 2 1

THE GUNSMITH

203

DEAD MAN'S BLUFF

ONE

Casey Tibbs had the smoothest skin Clint Adams had come across in a long time. Then again, she was in her early twenties, so why shouldn't it be smooth and clear and firm?

"What are you doing?" she asked with her face in the pillow. "It feels good."

He ran his fingertips over her skin once again.

"I'm examining the skin on your pretty ass," he said and ran a finger along the crease between her butt cheeks, up and down, up and down a few times.

"Mmmm," she said, wriggling her butt, "examine it some more."

"Okay," he said, leaning over her, "but I'm not going to use my fingers anymore. . . ."

"What is that?"

"My nose."

"And . . . that?"

"That's my tongue."

"Mmmmm . . . What's that?"

"My nose and tongue."

"Oh . . . ohhh . . . That's not your tongue. . . ."

"That's my hand," he said, sliding it beneath her so that

1

it lay flat against her stomach, between her tummy and the mattress.

"Roll over," he said huskily.

"Okay . . ."

She rolled over and he looked at her. She was tall and slender, with high, firm breasts, like ripe peaches. Her nipples were pink and large, and they fascinated him so much that he had spent a long time on them last night, just touching them, rubbing them, feeling them on the palm of his hand, beneath his tongue . . . until he drove Casey nearly crazy. She rolled him over then, mounted him, and took him inside and rode him hard until they were both spent and exhausted.

This morning he had started with her butt and now that she had turned over he was mesmerized by her breasts and nipples again, but he resisted. He didn't want her to think that her breasts were the only part of her body that he liked, because they weren't. Actually, right now that tawny patch of hair between her legs had caught his eyes. He ran his fingers through it, enjoying the way it felt between them, and then he found that she was already wet, and he slid his finger along her pink slit, gently going up and down, up and down while she moaned and began to alternately lift her butt off the bed and then grind it down into the bed. . . .

When he felt that she was near a climax he removed his hand and replaced it with his face. He rubbed his face in that patch of hair, then found her wetness again, this time with his lips and tongue.

"Oooh, God," she said, lifting her butt off the bed again and pressing her crotch hard against his face. His tongue worked avidly, his face grew wet with her juices, and finally she shuddered and began to beat on the bed with her fists. He mounted her quickly, even before her spasms subsided, and entered her. He took her hard, the way she had taken him the night before. He put one hand on either side of her to take his weight and simply drove himself in and out of her until his own spasms took over and he bellowed like a bull as he emptied himself into her. . . .

"One of us is going to break the other one at this rate," she said later, while she lay with her head on his shoulder.

He doubted it, as it was his intention to leave town that day.

"Oh, I know that's not true," she added. "You are, after all, leaving town today, aren't you?"

"Yes."

Clint had been in Blaisdell, Kansas, for almost five days—much too long. His intention when he arrived had been to stay a day or two, but then he'd met Casey, who worked in the general store, and his plans had changed . . . drastically.

Last night, however, he had decided once and for all that he had to leave town. He had to drag himself away from this lovely young woman who was just that, too young for him. She smelled fresh and clean all the time, and she glowed with a vitality that only came from youth. She was not even the *type* of woman he usually spent time with. She was too thin and—as he had already reminded himself time and again—too young. She was also looking for the kind of relationship that he couldn't provide.

"Yes," he said, "it's time to leave."

She rubbed her hand over his chest and said, "I'm glad you spent your last night in town with me."

"Who else would I spend it with?"

"I mean here in my room, and not at your hotel."

They had spent most of their nights together—and afternoons . . . and mornings—in his hotel room. For some reason, though, last night she had asked him to come home with her, and he'd agreed. It was there, while having some coffee, that he told her he was going to leave—and then they spent the night together.

"I'll make you some breakfast," she said, getting out of bed.

"You don't have to do that, Casey," he said.

"I know," she said, pulling on a dressing robe to cover her nakedness. She wasn't shy, just cold. "But I'd like to. May I?"

"Well, sure."

"Eggs?"

"That's fine."

There were only two rooms, the kitchen and this room, which had a bed and a chair in it, sort of a combination sitting room and bedroom.

There was a pitcher and basin in a corner and he used the water there to freshen up and get dressed. By the time he had picked up his gun belt he could smell the fresh coffee.

He carried the gun belt to the kitchen and hung it on the back of a chair, then sat. She put a plate of eggs and potatoes in front of him.

"I'm sorry, but I had no bacon."

"This is fine."

She sat opposite him with only a cup of coffee.

"You're not going to eat?" he asked.

"No," she said, "I'm going to watch you."

She had that look in her eyes, the one that said, "Wouldn't it be wonderful if I could watch you eat every morning for the rest of our lives?"

Yep, he definitely had to leave this morning.

TWO

When Clint left Casey's place he had to go back to his hotel to check out. From there he'd walk to the livery to reclaim his big black gelding, Duke. Once he left town he intended to ride south, into Texas and down to the town of Labyrinth, where he would stop and see his friend Rick Hartman.

He got as far as checking out of the hotel.

The three men saw Clint Adams enter his hotel that morning.

"It damn well is about time," one of them said, rubbing his bleary eyes with the fingers of one hand.

"You know," the second said, "taking on the Gunsmith with no sleep ain't smart."

The third man, who was in charge, said, "We don't have a choice. This has to be done today."

"Why didn't they send more men?" the first man complained.

"Yeah," the second man said. "After all, this is the Gunsmith we're talking about."

"The other men are equally as formidable," the leader said. "The Gunsmith is our part of the plan, and this has to be done today, or the timing will be off.''

"Them and their precious timing," the first man muttered.

"What?" the leader asked.

"Never mind," the first man said. "It wasn't important."

"When do we do this?" the second man asked. "And how?"

"We do it when he comes out," the leader said, "and in the street."

"Why don't we do it from a rooftop or something?" the first man asked.

"Because this is not about bushwhacking anybody," the leader said.

"What is this about?" the second man asked.

"Yeah?" the other chimed in. "I been wonderin' about that myself."

"That's not for you to know," the leader said, "or wonder about. You're getting paid to do as you're told, and you're getting paid a lot."

"He's got us there," the second man said to the first.

"Check your weapons," the leader said. "He'll be checking out, so he'll be coming back out soon."

All three men drew their guns, checked them, and returned them to their holsters. A few minutes earlier they'd been feeling tired and worn-out. Now they were just excited.

After all, they were going to kill the Gunsmith.

THREE

Bat Masterson examined his cards, then the man seated across from him, then his cards again. It had all come down to this hand. The game—a winner-take-all game—had started with two tables of eight players, and now there was only Bat and W.C. James. James was an unknown when the game started, as Bat had never played against him, met him, or even heard of him beforehand. In fact, James had started playing at the other table. This meant that all he knew about the man he had learned during the past nine hours.

The game was five-card stud. Bat had a king of hearts, queen of diamonds, and a pair of jacks showing, a club and a spade. In the hole he had another jack, this one hearts.

James was showing a ten, queen, king, and ace of hearts. He needed the jack for a straight flush, but Bat had it in the hole. However, any jack would have given him a straight, except that Bat had three of them. If the man had the fourth jack, he was the winner—if he stayed in the hand. The bet was Bat's, and he kept his eyes and hands still while he considered what the bet should be.

"Your bet, Bat," W.C. James said. Bat had heard a

friend of his call him "Carlos." The man had brought one friend with him, but the man was not allowed in the room while the game was going on, so he was out in the hotel saloon.

Bat had been in Denver a week, and much of the past two days—at least forty hours of them—had been spent right in this room.

"I'll bet five hundred," Bat said.

"Whew," James said, "pretty steep."

He was a tall, almost gaunt man, made to look even more so by hollowed-out cheeks. His skin had a leathery look, as if he'd led an outdoor life before becoming a gambler. He had a mane of salt-and-pepper hair combed straight back from his head and curling up over his collar.

The only other men allowed in the room were former players who had busted out of the game. They crowded around the room now, for what could be the last hand of the game.

"Five hundred to you, Mr. James," said Tyler Best, the host of the game. Tyler didn't play, but he loved organizing high-stakes games that went on for days.

Bat looked up at the men who were watching, then looked back at W.C. James.

"Five hundred," James said, counting the money out, "and a thousand more."

"He's got the royal," Bat heard someone whisper. He didn't need the royal, Bat thought, just the case jack, but in studying the man's face Bat suddenly became convinced that the man didn't have it. Not only that, he was convinced the man had aces. How he knew that was a mystery, but usually Bat's instincts were right—especially in a high-stakes game.

Bat had not seen W.C. James bluff. What he had seen for the past nine hours was a man who played the cards that were dealt to him. If he had a winning hand, he won. If he had a losing hand, he folded. And he had been riding an incredible streak of good luck—up until now.

"I'll call the thousand," Bat said, "and raise two."

James watched as Bat counted out the cash. There were no chips in this game. All the players had used real money.

"Quite a bet," James said.

He carefully counted out Bat's raise and then said, "And another three."

"You seem rather convinced about your hand, Mr. James," Bat said. "We've got about the same amount of money left. Let's see how convinced you are. I'll bet all of it."

Each player had bought in for five thousand and the play had started small, but had increased with each hour. That meant there was eighty thousand dollars on the table. Since there had already been about fifteen thousand in the pot, Bat's bet amounted to about thirty thousand, give or take.

The other men in the room "aaahed" and murmured and waited for W.C. James to make his play.

"Well," he said, "I can hardly back down now, can I?"

"Not if you've got me beat on the board, which I think you do," Bat said.

"Oh," James said, "I can beat jacks," and pushed his money into the center of the table.

"Bat?" Tyler Best said. "You're called."

Bat turned over the jack of hearts, effectively busting James's royal flush. It remained to be seen if the man had the last jack.

Everyone in the room held their breath, except Bat. He felt the man had an ace, and if he didn't—if he turned over the case jack—then Bat's instincts had failed him, and he had lost. He had lost poker games before, so there was no need to hold his breath. As high-stakes games went, this was not even the largest game he'd ever been in.

"Mr. James?" Tyler said.

W.C. James turned over his card, revealing an ace of clubs.

"He beat jacks, all right," Tyler said, "but not three of them. Bat wins."

Suddenly men were pounding Bat on the back and congratulating him. Bat ignored them until he could reach across the table and shake hands with W.C. James.

"Good game," he said.

James shook his hand and said, "I had a run of luck until that last hand. What made you so sure I didn't have the case jack?"

"Just a feeling," Bat said.

James shook his head.

"Wish I could get feelings like that."

"Bat?" Tyler Best asked. "How do you want your money?"

Bat looked at the man and said, "Just green, Tyler. Just green."

The two men sitting in the corner of the Denver House Saloon watched as the poker players trooped into the room, unshaven, bedraggled, but in good spirits.

"How can they all be so happy when only one of them wins?" the first man asked.

"It's not the winning and losing," the second man said, "it's playing the game that counts."

"Huh?" the first man asked. "What the hell's the point of playing if you don't win?"

"I guess that's why you're not a gambler."

They watched as Bat Masterson walked to the bar with a group of men and started buying drinks.

"I guess he won," the second man said. "He's doing the buying."

"Too bad," the first man said. "All that money is going to go to waste when we kill him."

FOUR

Heck Thomas looked up and down the tracks, and then down at the tracks themselves.

"What are you looking for?" The man speaking was Wesley Parsons, president of the new Pacific Coast Railroad.

"I won't know until I find it, Mr. Parsons," Thomas said.

"We're paying you for results, Mr. Thomas," Parsons said impatiently. "The wanton destruction of our track has got to stop. We can't afford to keep laying the same length of track over and over again."

"I realize that, Mr. Parsons," Thomas said. "You hired me because I'm the best in the business, didn't you?"

"That was what we were told," Parsons said, "although I had heard that Talbot Roper was the best private detective in the business."

"He is," Heck Thomas said without hesitation, "the best *private* detective. On the other hand, I'm the best *railroad* detective, and I believe that was what you were looking for."

"It was, indeed," Parsons said. "I stand corrected."

Parsons was a tall, barrel-chested man who, although he

13

had come west to build a railroad, still dressed as if he was in the East. Heck Thomas's clothes, however, were pure western wear. So it was that both men were rather dirty and grubby from walking the track; this did not bother Heck, but it fretted Parsons to no end.

"I am desperately in need of a bath," the railroad man said. "How much longer will this take?"

"I can't answer that, Mr. Parsons," Thomas said. "Perhaps you'd best go and have your bath and then join me further along the track."

"You'll still be walking the track when I'm done?" Parsons asked, surprised.

"I'll be walking this track until I find something that will help me, Mr. Parsons."

Parsons cleared his throat and said grudgingly, "Well, no one can claim that you are not conscientious."

"No, sir," Heck Thomas agreed. "Nobody has ever been able to claim that."

"Very well," Parsons said. "I'll go back to Sacramento and freshen up, and then I will rejoin you."

"Fine," Thomas said, although it was more than fine. The last thing he wanted was to have this eastern dude breathing down his neck the whole time he was trying to do his job. "I'll see you then."

And he continued to walk the track while Parsons retraced his steps to the buggy and driver he had hired to bring him out here.

"What's he lookin' for?" the first man asked.

"Damned if I know," said the second man.

"Harkey?" the first man said, addressing the third man.

"I don't know," Harkey said, "and I don't care. We're not being paid to worry about what he's lookin' for. We're bein' paid to kill him."

"We know that," the first man said.

"We was just wonderin', is all," the second man said.

"Well, stop wonderin'."

The other two men fell into a wounded sort of silence and continued to watch the two men below them walk the track.

"Hey, what's this?" the first man asked.

They saw the well-dressed eastern-looking man turn and walk away, while Heck Thomas continued to walk up the track, leading his horse, head down as he studied the tracks for who knew what.

"The other man is leavin'," said Harkey. "This is our chance."

"What's the worry about witnesses?" the first man asked.

"We ain't worried about witnesses," Harkey said.

"Then why couldn't we kill him while he was with that other fella?" the second man asked.

"Look," Harkey said, "I'm the one got the orders, and I'm the one givin' the orders to you. All you fellas have to do is what I tell you to do. Got it?"

"We got it," the first man said.

The second man nodded.

Harkey had no doubt that he could kill Heck Thomas. He just wished he hadn't been saddled with two sad specimens like these two. They always had to know why something was bein' done, when all they had to do was take orders.

"Come on," he said.

"Where we goin'?" the first one asked.

Harkey sighed.

"We're gonna ride up track some so that we're all set up when he gets there."

They followed Harkey to where they had tied off their horses.

"Why don't we just take care of him now?" the second man asked.

Harkey turned and glared at him.

"I know," the man said. "We just got to do what we're told."

"So if you know that," Harkey said, "why don't you shut up and just do what you're bein' paid to do?"

With that they all mounted up, the first two men once again maintaining a wounded silence.

When this job was over, Harkey thought, he was going to find two better men to team with.

FIVE

Clint paid his bill, hung his saddlebag over his left shoulder, carried his rifle in that hand, and left the hotel, heading for the livery.

"Clint Adams!" a voice called.

Clint stopped short and looked down at the ground. He'd heard his name spoken in that tone so many times before that he knew what was coming—and dreaded it.

"Adams!" the voice called again. "Turn around."

It was early enough in the morning that the streets were pretty empty. That was the only blessing here. No innocent bystanders would be hurt—that is, if gawkers who were on the lookout for blood could ever be called "innocent bystanders."

Clint turned and saw that he was facing three men. He waited to see which one was the spokesman. That was usually the man he'd have to kill first.

"You *are* Clint Adams, aren't you?" the man in the center asked.

"That's right."

"I guess you know what we're here for."

"Well," Clint said, "if you're no different from every other damn fool I seem to run across, yeah, I know why you're here."

"Who you callin' a fool?" the man on the left asked, scowling.

These three were of a kind. The only difference in them was that the man in the middle, the spokesman, was five or six years older than the other two, who appeared to be in their twenties.

"You," Clint said, "and your two friends here. Damn fools are the only ones I know who want to die before breakfast."

"How's he know we ain't had breakfast yet?" the man on the right asked.

"Shut up!" the spokesman said. "Let's get this over with, Adams."

"In this situation," Clint said, "I'd usually try to talk you out of this."

"Sorry," the man said, "can't do that."

Clint frowned.

"Can't or won't?"

"We been paid—" the man on the right said. But the spokesman silenced him with a clipped "Quiet!"

"Paid?" Clint asked. "Somebody's paying you to die, boy?"

The two flanking men remained silent.

"Don't matter why we're doing it, Adams," the man in the center said. "Just that we do it."

"You're wrong there, friend," Clint said. "You don't have to do this. Nobody can be paying you enough money to die for."

"You stallin', Adams?" the man asked. "Hoping maybe somebody'll bring the sheriff?"

"That would be nice," Clint said. "Maybe a lawman would be able to talk some sense into you three."

"Not likely," the man said.

"You do this for a living, friend?" Clint asked. "Kill people?"

"I've killed some."

"What about you two?" Clint asked the others. "You kill people for money before? Ever killed *anybody* before?"

They didn't answer, but one was biting his lip and the other one was flexing his hand over and over.

"No," Clint said, "I don't think you have."

"That's enough talk, Adams."

"You going to let him decide whether you live or die?" Clint asked the others.

"Let's go, Adams."

Clint looked at the man in the middle.

"You going to let me put aside my saddlebags and rifle?" he asked.

"What for?" the man asked. "Your gun hand is free."

And he went for his gun.

SIX

"Do we have to do this here?" the first man asked. "In front of witnesses?"

"No," the second man said, "we'll wait for him to go outside."

"Good."

They settled in to watch and wait for Bat Masterson to finish at the bar and leave the Denver House Saloon.

Bat Masterson stood at the bar with several of the players from the tournament, including W.C. James, the man he beat in the final hand.

"Nice of you to buy drinks, Bat," James said, "especially since you're using my money."

"And mine," another man said.

"And mine," a third chimed in.

"Never let it be said I'm not generous with other people's money," Bat said.

One by one the other players finished their drinks and left, leaving Bat with W.C. James.

"Tell me something?" James asked.

"Sure, what?"

"What made you so sure I didn't have the jack?" the

man asked. "I mean, I know you had three of them, and the odds were against me having it, but I *could* have had it."

"Yes, you could have," Bat said, "but for some reason I knew you didn't."

"You just . . . felt it?"

"That's right."

James shook his head.

"That's the kind of instinct for this game I'd kill to have," he said.

"Play it long enough," Bat said, "and it will come to you." James was not much younger than Bat, but it was as if an older man were imparting wisdom to a much younger one.

"I hope so," James said. "Another drink? I'll buy this time."

"No thanks," Bat said. "I got a lot of money in my pocket. I don't want to end up spending it on whiskey and women, or worse, get into another poker game. I'm going to go for a walk to clear my head, and then turn in."

"When are you leaving Denver?"

"In the morning."

"Well," James said, extending his hand, "it was a pleasure watching you work."

"We'll see each other across a poker table again someday," Bat said. "Of that I'm sure."

Bat turned and walked away from the bar. The two men sitting in the corner watched his progress. He had two choices. He could go through the door that led to the hotel lobby or the one that led outside.

"What do we do if he goes to his room?" the first man asked.

"What we have to do," the second said.

But he didn't go into the hotel, he went directly outside.

"This is it," the second man said, "let's go."

The two men got up from their table and hurried outside.

Bat was walking down the street at a leisurely pace, his intention being to simply circle the block and walk into the hotel by the front door. Denver always felt different to Bat. He never expected the things that happened in the streets of Dodge and Abilene to happen in the streets of Denver.

But everybody's wrong sometime.

"Masterson!"

He heard his name shouted from behind, and it was not the shout of a friend.

The two men from the hotel were already drawing their guns as Bat turned. Apparently, they weren't prepared to bushwhack him, but a completely fair fight was out of the question. The shout was simply meant to turn him around so that he wasn't found shot in the back.

But Bat's hand was moving, too, as he turned. His gun was in a shoulder holster, which he favored when he was in one of the larger cities like San Francisco or Denver. As the gun cleared leather he fell into a crouch. One of the men got off a shot first, but it went over Bat's head. It was dusk, so darkness was not a problem yet. Had the two men waited a few more minutes, darkness might have been on their side.

Bat fired once and the first man clutched at his chest and went down. The second man, gun in hand, turned to run, but he turned right into W.C. James's gun, which barked once, putting the man down.

Bat and James met right between the two dead men.

"Much obliged," Bat said.

"I saw them leave the saloon in a hurry, right after you," James said. "I thought there might be trouble."

Bat examined each of the men and found them both dead.

"I don't understand," James said.

"What don't you understand?"

"Well, if their aim was to rob you, why call out to you to make you turn around? Why not try to get you in an alley or something? Or simply follow you to your room?"

"Well," Bat said, replacing the spent shell in his gun with a live one and then holstering the weapon, "I guess robbery wasn't their intention."

"Then what?"

"Maybe they just wanted to kill me."

"Why?"

Bat shrugged and said, "Reputation."

"I guess that happens to you a lot."

"More than I care to mention," Bat said. "Still, the way they did it . . ."

Bat leaned over and began going through the men's pockets.

"Should be a policeman along here pretty soon," James warned.

"Well, you're my witness that they started it," Bat said. "I just want to see who they were."

He went through their pockets and didn't find anything.

"Nothing?"

"No identification," Bat said, "but there is this."

He came out of one man's pocket with a wad of cash.

"That's a lot of money, Bat."

"I guess robbery definitely is out of the question," Bat said.

He put the money back. There was one more pocket to check and he found something in it.

"What's this?" he asked, straightening up.

"Looks like a business card."

Both stared at the card, and what was on it, totally puzzled.

SEVEN

Men like Heck Thomas lived their entire adult lives by instinct. It's what kept them alive. Thomas had seen it in many men before, like his friend Clint Adams, and also his colleague Talbot Roper. Unquestioning, they followed their instincts.

Heck Thomas walked the tracks of the Pacific Coast Railroad, but his instincts were shouting at him that he was being watched.

It was quiet where he was, so quiet he could hear himself breathing, hear his horse snort every so often—and hear other things. Horses made all kinds of sounds, and so did men, many of them unintentional, and if you listened hard enough—or had the instincts—those sounds came to you even without your knowing it.

Heck Thomas couldn't say how or why, but he knew he was being watched, and knew it was by more than one person.

The job he'd been hired for was to find out who was fooling with the PCR's tracks, fouling them and, in some cases, demolishing them. Up to now, though, there had been no violence involved with the vandalism and—after listening to Wesley Parsons's story—Heck was convinced that there would be no violence.

So if he was being watched by the vandals, he didn't think he needed to be fearful in any way. However, if he was being watched by someone else—bandits or drifters or someone who had recognized him and wanted to pad their own reputation with his—then he had to be careful.

Anyone watching him would think he was concentrating completely on the tracks at his feet.

"He's lost in those tracks," one of the men said.

"Maybe," Harkey said.

"Look at him," the second man said. "He ain't even looked up once."

Harkey wasn't convinced. A man like Heck Thomas did not get a reputation by ever being completely engrossed in anything.

"Why don't we do it?" the first man said.

"From here?" Harkey asked.

"I could take him with a rifle from here," the second man said.

"No," Harkey said, "no ambush."

"A fair fight?" the first man asked.

"That's the way it has to be."

"Three against one?" the second man asked.

"That's as fair as he gets," Harkey said. "Come on, we'll just ride down there and do it."

Heck Thomas heard the horses and knew he'd been right. As nonchalantly as he could, he turned his horse so that the shotgun on his saddle was within his reach. Then he turned to look at the approaching horses. There were three of them, two riding behind one—the leader. They all wore ragged trail clothes and guns that had seen a lot of use.

Thomas waited until they were within range of the shotgun.

"That's far enough."

The men reined in.

"What's wrong, friend?" the leader asked.

"I ain't your friend," Thomas said, "and you been watching me for the better part of half an hour. What's on your mind?"

The man shifted in his saddle, then settled back down on it.

"Watching you?" he asked. "What makes you think we been watching you?"

"You make a lot of noise, especially when you're trying not to."

"What's he mean—" one of the other men started to ask, but the leader waved him silent. The two men with him fanned out so that they weren't right behind him.

"My name's Heck Thomas," the railroad detective said. "Are you sure you're looking for me?"

"We're sure," the leader said.

"Well, then, get to it, friend," Thomas said. "I ain't got all day."

"Ain't nothin' personal in this, friend," the man said.

"It's personal to me," Thomas said.

He kept his eye on the leader's eyes. They widened a split second before he went for his gun. Thomas's hand flashed for the shotgun and he cleared leather and brought it around in one, quick fluid motion. He pulled the trigger. The load of heavy shot yanked the leader right from his saddle, as if he'd been pulled from behind. Thomas dropped the shotgun and hit the ground, rolling and drawing his gun. The other two men recovered from the shock of seeing their leader killed, but not quickly enough. Thomas came to a stop on one knee and fired three times. His first shot was hasty and struck one of the horses, but his next two shots were true and both men fell from their saddles.

Thomas remained on one knee, waiting and listening. If there were any more men up in the hills he wanted to be able to hear them coming. After a few moments he had satisfied himself that there weren't any more, and he stood up. He walked to the three men and when he was sure they were dead he ejected the spent shells from his gun and loaded in live ones. Then he walked to the shotgun, retrieved it, and did the same thing. He returned it to its place on his saddle and walked to the dead men. He began to search their pockets for identification but came away empty. Each man, however, had an unusual amount of money in his pockets.

They'd been paid for this.

He continued his search and found something interesting in the vest pocket of the leader. It looked like a business card, but the character in the center of it made him frown as he tried to figure out what the hell was going on.

EIGHT

Sometimes a man just becomes convinced he wants to die, and there's nothing you can do to stop him. In this instance there were three of them, and they left Clint no choice.

Clint had seen a man face three men in a gunfight once. The one man killed the three, and he did it by fanning his gun. Clint never found out the man's name, and never heard of a man doing that before or since. Fanning a weapon and firing it accurately is difficult, because as the side of your hand strikes the hammer to push it back, you're also jerking the barrel of the gun upward. He had watched the man carefully, and as he fanned his weapon the barrel was almost pointing straight down to the ground. When the edge of his hand struck the hammer, forcing it back it also forced the gun up into firing position.

Clint had always admired the way that man had fanned his gun, and to this day wished he knew who the man was. He didn't, though, and he never found out, so he was never able to talk to the man about fanning a weapon accurately.

Even if Clint could have fanned his gun accurately it wouldn't have helped him now. His rifle was in his left hand, and his saddlebags were over his left shoulder, so both were encumbering his left hand. However, since Clint's weapon was a double-action Colt—modified by his own hand—he didn't need to fan the weapon to fire it quickly—which was, after all, the whole point of fanning a gun.

Clint needed only to draw and pull the trigger three times, very quickly, to dispatch the three men. It was a testament to how much faster he was than them that all of that information about "fanning" went through his mind before he killed them.

Even on a quiet morning gunfire brings people onto the street, and now they began to pour from the hotel, the cafés, from people's homes—and from the sheriff's office.

Clint had met the sheriff the first day he came to town. The man's name was Rutherford Hayes and, oddly, his friends called him "Ruth." By the second day in town, Clint was also calling him by that name.

"What's going on, Clint?" Hayes asked. "Thought you were leaving today."

"I was, Ruth," Clint said. He ejected empties from his gun and loaded it with live rounds again before holstering it. He had already checked the three men to see if they were dead. They were.

"Who are these three?" the sheriff asked.

"I don't know," Clint said. "I never saw them before."

"And they just braced you out of the blue?"

"Just as I left the hotel to go to the livery."

"They must've been crazy."

Hayes looked around and beckoned to two men, who stepped forward.

"Grab a few others. I'll need help clearing these three out of the street."

"Sure, Sheriff."

Hayes looked at Clint again.

"Reputation seekers, ya think?"

"I thought that at first, Ruth," Clint said, "but one of them said they'd been paid."

Hayes's eyes widened.

"Somebody *paid* them to die today?"

"Looks like it. Can we go through their pockets? See if they have anything with their names on it?"

"Sure," Hayes said.

"You'd better do it, Ruth," Clint said. "You're the law, and there's a crowd."

"Right."

While Hayes searched through the pockets of the dead men, Clint walked to where he'd dropped his rifle and saddlebags. As he retrieved them Casey came rushing from the hotel. She saw him and ran into his arms.

"When I heard the gunfire I knew it was you," she said. "Are you all right?"

"Sure, he's all right, missy," a man standing nearby said. "He's the Gunsmith, and there was only three of 'em."

A few men started to laugh until Clint silenced them with a glare.

"I'm fine, Casey."

"What did they want?"

"Apparently, they were hired to kill me."

"Who would hire them?"

"I don't know, offhand," Clint said. "If I took the time, though, I could probably come up with a few names."

"Clint?"

He turned as the sheriff approached him.

"This is what they had in their pockets."

The sheriff was holding a lot of money in his hands, and what looked like a business card.

"That's it?" Clint asked. "Nothing with their names on it?"

"Nope."

"That's a lot of money."

"Supports what you said about them being paid."

"Paid a lot," Clint said, "and in advance. Better use that to bury them."

"There's more here than that."

"Donate it to the town's treasury. What's that?"

"I don't know," Hayes said, "but it's odd looking."

Clint took it from the sheriff's hand. It not only looked like a business card, it was, but there weren't any names on it. The only thing on it was a big circle, centered, and inside the circle was the number nine, also centered.

"What does it mean, Clint?"

Clint frowned at it and said, "I haven't the faintest idea."

NINE

The incident kept Clint in Blaisdell a little longer. He wanted to try to find out who the men were, thereby possibly finding out who had hired them. He was used to gunmen wanting to try him in the street when they recognized him, but finding out that they were hired to kill him, that was something else.

Three extra days in town didn't help, though, and he finally left and rode straight to Labyrinth, Texas. If anyone could help him with this problem, it was Rick Hartman, who had connections all over the country.

Things changed in Labyrinth while he was gone, but they stayed the same, too. Although the name of the hotel he used had changed—he didn't even remember what it was called the last time he was there, but someone had finally smacked LABYRINTH HOUSE on it—they still saved the same room for him. Rick Hartman's influence, he was sure.

"Glad to have you with us, Mr. Adams," the clerk said.

"It's nice to be back in town . . . uh . . ."

"Philip."

"Right, Philip."

"I wasn't here the last time you were in town, but I know who you are. Everyone does."

Which wasn't necessarily a good thing, but it didn't seem to matter much in Labyrinth.

"Here's your key. Same room, of course."

"Thank you."

Clint went up to the room to drop off his saddlebags and rifle, then came back down and left the hotel. He had sent Rick a telegram from Blaisdell, so that he could begin working on the problem during the time it took Clint to get there. Hopefully, he had some answers by now.

The one thing in town that never changed was Rick's Place, Rick Hartman's saloon and gambling establishment. Oh, the girls changed, and the bartenders changed, but Rick was always there, and he was always glad to see Clint.

"You stayed away too long this time," Rick scolded him as they shook hands.

Clint didn't know what to say to that. He sat down as the bartender brought over a beer for him.

"Clint, this is Winston."

Clint looked at the tall, powerfully built man in his late forties. He had a square chin, salt-and-pepper hair, and incredibly white teeth.

"Mr. Adams," the man said, in a voice so low it sounded like thunder.

"Call me Clint, Winston."

The two men shook hands and Winston went back behind the bar. It was mid-afternoon, so there was no gambling going on and the place was less than a quarter full.

"So?" Clint asked, after sipping the beer. "Come up with anything?"

"Maybe," Rick said, "but you aren't going to like it."

"Somebody hired three men to kill me, Rick," Clint said. "I already don't like it."

"You know Carney Baker?"

"I know Carney," Clint said. "He's a good hand with a gun."

"Pete Miller?"

Clint nodded. He was starting to get a bad feeling about this.

"I know Miller's rep."

"And Walt Gordon?"

"I met Gordon once. He's a fast hand."

"They're all dead."

Clint narrowed his eyes.

"Tell me the rest."

"Where's that card?"

Clint knew what he meant. He took out the card with the circle on it, put it on the table, right in the center, where they could both see it clearly.

"In all three cases—Baker, Gordon, and Miller—the undertaker or the local lawman found one of those in their pocket."

Clint reached out and touched the card, but didn't pick it up.

"Somebody's sending a message," he said. "How were they killed?"

"Some sort of gunfight. None of them were ambushed, but they were all outnumbered—like you were."

"What the hell is going on?" Clint wondered out loud. "What's a nine in a circle mean?"

"I don't know," Rick said, "but I'm still checking. Stay around for a while. I can watch your back while we wait for some answers."

That didn't seem like a bad idea. Hell, there was nowhere else to go. He didn't know where to look for the answers; he might as well sit tight and see if the answers came to him.

"Okay," Clint said, "okay, I'll stay around for a while."

"Good," Rick said. "Maybe I can even get up a decent game of poker."

TEN

Clint got more information about the deaths of Baker, Gordon, and Miller from Rick.

Carney Baker had met his end in the streets of Parks, Nevada, a little nothing of a town where he had fallen on hard times. He'd taken a job as shotgun at a small gambling saloon there, so when three men came in and braced him it looked like a personal argument. The law there claimed he could have walked away from it, but Clint knew better. One, Baker wasn't the type, and two—judging by his own experience—the three men were not about to let him walk away. He killed one of the men, wounded another, but in the end he was killed and buried on Boot Hill with no marker.

Pete Miller came to his end outside a whorehouse in Mexico City, down in Old Mexico. Two men, this time, and they seemed to be waiting for him when he came out. Miller had his gun belt slung over his shoulder, and the two men who braced him did not allow him to strap it on. He was at a disadvantage, and he paid for it.

Walt Gordon was in San Francisco and got into a fight that was apparently over a woman at one of the Portsmouth Square gambling parlors. He stepped outside, ostensibly to settle the matter, and found himself facing three men instead of one. He killed one, and the others killed him.

Three men who made their living—or, at least, their reputations—with guns killed under the oddest of situations. And of course the oddest thing of all was the business card with the Circle-Nine, found on all of them.

"Do you know what I'm thinking?" Clint asked.

"What?" Rick asked.

"What if these three instances were the successful ones?" Clint asked. "What if there were others, like me, who weren't killed?"

"Could be," Rick said. "How do we find out?"

"I'd like to see what the newspapers had on these three killings," Clint said.

"I thought you might," Rick said. "I found some. They're in my office—at least, the ones I could get ahold of. The Austin paper carried the story of Gordon being killed in San Francisco. They also had the one about Miller."

"Way ahead of me, huh?"

"Maybe more than you think."

"What's that mean?"

"It means I know you," Rick said. "You're not only upset about what happened to you, but about what happened to Baker, Miller, and Gordon."

"It shouldn't have happened," Clint said.

"You're thinking some kind of conspiracy."

"Well, what are you thinking?" Clint asked. "The same business card shows up at all three of those murders, and at the attempt on me."

"Murders?"

"What would you call them?"

"Most onlookers called them fair fights. What would yours have been called?"

"A fair fight," Clint said, "if you can count three to one fair."

"When the one is you most people would," Rick said.

"Well, it's not," Clint said, "no matter who the one is. What if someone is out to get rid of us?"

"Who's us?"

"Men—people—with reputations for being good with a gun."

"And why would someone want to do that, Clint?"

"I don't know," Clint said, "but I'm going to find out."

"I knew you were going to say that. Are you going to stay around long enough for us to get some information?" "Sure," Clint said, "but I'm going to be sending out some telegrams of my own."

"To who?"

"Bat, Wyatt, Frank Leslie, Ben Thompson, some of the others."

"To see if this has happened to them?"

"Right, and if it hasn't to warn them that it might."

"Sounds like a good idea," Rick said. "You want to look at those newspapers now?"

"Sure."

"Take a fresh beer and go into my office. I'm going to stay out here. We're going to start getting busy in a little while."

"Fine." Clint stood up. "Rick, thanks for your help."

"You knew I'd help."

"Well, thanks for not thinking I'm crazy."

Rick smiled.

"It's not that I don't think you're crazy," he said, "but I can't come up with any other explanations right now."

"Well, whatever the reasons," Clint said, "I appreciate your help."

"I'm always here, and always ready to help."

Clint went to the bar, got a fresh beer from Winston, and carried it back to Rick's office with him.

ELEVEN

Over the course of the next few days Clint sent out telegrams, trying to locate friends like Bat Masterson and Wyatt Earp, Jake Benteen and Fred Hammer, others who—like himself—were known for their prowess with a gun. Some he located, some he didn't. The ones he could find he questioned, and then warned. The one that concerned him most was Bat Masterson. He couldn't seem to locate him, and no one had any word on where he'd last been seen.

Clint hadn't sent a warning to Luke Short, because Luke was known more for his gambling than his gun. However, since he was trying to find Bat, he decided to try to see if Luke might know where he was. He received a telegram in return:

HEARD FROM ED THAT BAT WAS GOING TO DENVER FOR A GAME STOP HAVEN'T HEARD FROM EITHER SINCE STOP TROUBLE STOP

LUKE SHORT

Clint knew that if he told Luke yes, there was trouble, Luke would be on his way—but to where? There was no point in alarming his friend if there was nothing else to tell him, so he sent back a telegram he hoped was somewhat neutral. He told Luke that at the first sign of trouble he would let him know.

Now all he had to do was locate Bat Masterson or his brother Ed.

"Where's he supposed to be?" Rick Hartman asked.

"Who knows?" Clint asked. "The last place he was supposed to be was Denver, for a poker game."

"And what do you know about that?"

"Nothing."

"So how can you find out?"

"By asking somebody."

"And who do you know in Denver you could ask?"

Clint stared at Rick, feeling stupid, then left Rick's Place and went back to the telegraph office.

Clint felt even dumber when he received the reply from Talbot Roper in Denver.

> BAT HERE FOR GAME DAYS AGO STOP ATTEMPT MADE ON STREET UNSUCCESSFUL STOP NO OTHER INFOR- MATION STOP
>
>   ROPER

Which was more information than he'd had before. Bat had been in Denver for a game, and there had been an attempt to kill him. Clint still needed to locate Bat to ask about the Circle-Nine business card.

•   •   •

Rick gave Clint back the telegram.

"Maybe this just means you're not thinking straight," he said, "or you would have come up with Roper, yourself."

Clint frowned. If it was true he wasn't thinking straight, what could he do about it?

"Why does this have you so frazzled?" Rick asked. "People have tried to kill you before."

"I don't like it when people are hired to kill me," Clint said, "and my friends . . . and then I find out that it's . . ."

"A conspiracy?"

"I don't want to sound paranoid," Clint said, "but look at the facts. Baker, Miller, Gordon, all dead. Attempts made on me and Bat."

"What about Wyatt?"

"Haven't located him. He might still be tracking the men who killed Morgan."

"Still some repercussions from that whole O.K. Corral thing?"

"Looks like."

"So maybe he's safe, then. Did you find Frank Leslie? Ben Thompson?"

"No attempts made on them, but Ben is known more for his gambling."

"Isn't Bat?"

"I would have thought so, but remember he's been a lawman."

"If it was just you," Rick said, "would you be this upset?"

"I—"

"I'll answer that for you," Rick said, interrupting. "No, you wouldn't. You don't like it that someone might be killing your friends, too."

"No, I don't."

"And you're going to do something about it."

"Right."

"Even if nobody else is."

"Especially if no one else is."

"What are you going to do?"

"I don't know yet."

"I have a suggestion."

"Which is?"

"Stay here and do nothing."

Clint looked at his friend.

"What would that accomplish, Rick?"

"If you're right about all this," Rick said, "it will happen again."

"So?"

"When it does, go to wherever it happens. The trail will be fresh."

"You mean, wait for someone else to die?"

Now Rick stared at Clint.

"When," he said finally, "you say it like that it just sounds silly."

"No, wait," Clint said, "you might have a point here."

"I do? Which point?"

"Going to the last place it happened," Clint said, "the place where the trail is warmest."

"Where would that be?"

"Well, according to the newspaper account I saw," Clint said, "San Francisco."

"Walt Gordon."

"Right."

"And you certainly know your way around San Francisco."

"Yes, I do."

"Makes as much sense to me as anything," Rick said.

"That's what I'll do, then," Clint said. "Tomorrow I'll head for San Francisco."

"You could use somebody to watch your back."

"You want to go to San Francisco?"

Rick just stared at him. He'd left Labyrinth once in the past five or six years, and that was to go on a gambling train with Clint—a trip that did not turn out very well.

"I'll just have to find someone when I get there, then," Clint said.

"Send me a telegram when you get there, let me know where you're staying," Rick said. "By that time I might have some more information for you."

"At least I'll be doing something," Clint said, "which will be a hell of a lot better than just sitting around here, waiting for someone else to die."

"Okay, okay," Rick said, "it was a bad idea. I admit it."

"You should buy me a beer, to make up for it."

"I should buy you a beer," Rick said, signaling to Winston, the bartender. "Like today is any different than any other day?"

Clint sat back and relaxed, deciding to enjoy the quiet moment. It might be his last for a long time.

TWELVE

When Clint got to San Francisco he checked into the Alhambra in Portsmouth Square. He usually stayed at a hotel outside of the Square, but this time he decided to stay right in the middle of everything. Besides, the Alhambra was where Walt Gordon had been staying when he was killed.

He was not well known at the Alhambra—not on sight, anyway, but when he registered the clerk's face betrayed the fact that he recognized the name. Most of the clerks who worked the hotels in Portsmouth Square recognized well-known names or the names of the high rollers.

"Welcome to the Alhambra, Mr. Adams."

"Thanks."

"Is there anything special we could do for you during your stay?"

"Other than giving me a room, just one thing."

"And what would that be?"

"I'd like to talk to whoever runs your gambling operation."

"That would be our Mr. Frate."

"Fine," Clint said. "Would you let him know I'd like to talk to him, and then let me know when he's available?"

47

"Of course, sir," the clerk said. "Would you like him to come to your room?"

"That won't be necessary," Clint said. "Does he have an office?"

"Yes, sir."

"If I could see him there that would be fine."

"Very good, sir," the man said, "I'll see to it."

"What's your name?"

"Harold, sir." Harold was in his early thirties, with a little, well-cared-for mustache and slicked down, shiny black hair. "I am the head desk clerk."

Clint wondered what the next rung on the ladder was for a head desk clerk.

"It's a very great pleasure to meet you, Mr. Adams," Harold said, apparently breaking with protocol. He put out his hand and Clint accepted it. "You're the second man today it's been my pleasure to meet."

"Really?"

"Yes, sir. I've read so much about both of you."

"And who would the other one be?"

For his answer Harold glanced around to see if anyone was looking, then turned the register around so Clint could read for himself the name he was pointing to.

"Bat Masterson," Harold said. "Do you know him?"

"Oh, yes," Clint said, nodding his head, "I know him very well."

When Bat Masterson opened his door Clint was standing there holding the Circle-Nine business card up so Bat could see it. Bat immediately took one from his pocket and showed it to Clint.

"Why doesn't this surprise me?" Bat asked.

"You want to talk up here or have a drink?"

"Oh, a drink," Bat said. "Definitely a drink."

They went downstairs.

THIRTEEN

Bat Masterson was insulted.

"They sent three men after you? Three after Gordon? Only two after me?"

"Maybe you're better known for your gambling."

"Don't try to appease me, Clint," he said. "When we find out who's behind this they're going to pay for this insult."

"Is that what we're going to do? Find out who is behind it?"

"Why else would you be here? Why else would I be here?" Bat asked.

"To gamble."

"Well, let's hope that's what they think—whoever they are."

"Why did you come here?"

"Because of Gordon," Bat said. "I mean, because this was the most recent of the killings."

"Where did you find your card?" Clint asked.

"In the pocket of one of the men I killed," Bat said. "Well, actually, the man Carlos killed."

"Carlos?"

"W.C. James. I mentioned him."

He hadn't mentioned that his name was "Carlos" but that was beside the point.

"I found mine on one of them, too," Clint said, "but the others were found in the pockets of Gordon, Miller, and Baker."

"Did anyone see the killers put them there?"

"I don't know," Clint said. "One of the things I wanted to do when I got here was check the newspapers. There's bound to be more in the San Francisco papers than was in the papers in Austin and Labyrinth."

"Well," Bat said, "that'll be your job. I'm not going to spend time going through newspapers."

"What are you going to do?"

"I haven't decided yet."

"I'm trying to get an appointment to speak with the man who runs the gambling operation here," Clint said. "His name's Frate."

"Donald Frate?"

"I don't know his first name," Clint said. "You know him?"

"I know of him," Bat said. "He's run some operations before, but never one as big as this."

"Does he know you?"

"Not personally."

"You know friends of Gordon?"

"Maybe," Bat said. "I know a lot of people in town. I could probably find out who his friends were."

"Maybe that's where you should start, then. It might be helpful to be able to talk to some of his friends."

"What do you think is going on, Clint?"

"I'll tell you what Rick Hartman thinks of what I think," Clint said. "He thinks I'm paranoid."

"Conspiracy?"

Clint nodded.

"Against men like you and me?" Bat asked. "Walt Gordon—wait a minute. What about Wyatt and some of the others?''

"I can't get ahold of Wyatt, but I've checked in with Frank Leslie, Ben Thompson, and some others. No attempts yet.''

"When were Baker, Miller, and Gordon killed?''

"Baker and Miller after the attempts on you and me, Gordon after—but they were all only days apart.''

Bat frowned.

"I'd say they started at the top with you and me, but the others weren't in our league,'' Bat observed immodestly.

"But who is?''

"True.''

They raised their beers to each other and drank. Clint was about to say something else when he noticed the head desk clerk, Harold, enter the saloon. When he spotted Clint he brightened and came walking over.

"Mr. Adams, so glad to have found you,'' he said. "Hello, Mr. Masterson.''

"Harold.''

"Mr. Adams, I have a message from our Mr. Frate.''

"Yes?''

"He'd be happy to entertain you in his office in''—the man paused to check his pocket watch—''fifty minutes, if that's convenient.''

"That's very convenient, Harold,'' Clint said. "Tell Mr. Frate I said thank you.''

"Yes, sir. I'll do that. Gentlemen.''

As Harold walked away Bat said, "He's the head desk clerk, you know.''

"So he told me.''

"What's next, do you think?''

"Manager, I guess—or assistant manager.''

"What about that?''

"What?''

"Talking to the manager of the hotel."

"Why don't you see if you can do that while I talk to Frate," Clint suggested.

"All right. After that I'll check with some of the people I know about Gordon's friends. Let's meet for dinner and compare notes."

"Where?"

"Delmonico's?"

"At seven?" Clint asked.

Bat nodded and they both stood up.

"I'm glad you're here, Bat," Clint said. "I was wondering who was going to watch my back."

"Don't get mushy on me, Clint," Bat said, "but I'm glad you're here, too."

The two men shook hands warmly and left the saloon.

FOURTEEN

Clint appeared at the office door of the hotel's Mr. Frate fifty-four minutes later and knocked.

"Come in."

Clint entered and saw a man standing behind a small desk—or perhaps the desk seemed small because the man was so large. He was well over six feet, with broad shoulders, narrow hips, black hair slicked down and unparted, well dressed in a black suit and boiled white shirt. He appeared to be in his early forties.

He smiled and asked, "Mr. Clint Adams?"

"That's right."

"Come in, sir," Frate said. "I am Donald Frate, the casino manager."

Clint approached the desk. It did not escape his notice that Frate remained where he was and made Clint come to him. The two shook hands.

"Please, have a seat," Frate said, seating himself. Clint sat down in a chair that had been placed directly opposite the man. Frate seemed to make as few moves as possible.

"Our head desk clerk told me you wanted to speak to me about something."

"That's right."

"What can I do for you?"

"I'm interested in what happened to Walt Gordon while he was here."

"That was a terrible tragedy," Frate said, his brows knitting together, "terrible. Mr. Gordon was a regular and a valued customer—but I must correct you on one thing."

"Oh, yes?"

"Indeed. You see, he wasn't killed *here*. He was killed outside."

"But I understood the argument started here."

"It may well have," Frate said, "but it escalated into tragedy outside. Do you see my point?"

"I think I do. You're saying that the hotel had no liability in what happened."

"The casino," he said, "but yes, you see my point."

"And it's well taken," Clint said. "I'm not here to assign blame to anyone."

"Why are you here, then . . . if I may ask?"

"I simply have a few questions that need to be answered."

"I see. And was Mr. Gordon a friend of yours?"

"Let's say . . . a colleague."

"I believe I understand," Frate said. "Well, ask your questions, and I only hope I can be of some help."

But now that Clint was sitting face-to-face with Frate, he wasn't sure what to ask. He knew he had to come up with something, though, or look foolish.

"Did Mr. Gordon have any other altercations while he was here?"

"Not that I know of," Frate said, then held up his hand and added, "that is, inside the casino."

"I understand."

"I would have no knowledge of what went on outside," Frate added unnecessarily.

"Yes, I understand. The men who, uh, Walt Gordon had

the, uh, altercation with. Had they ever been here before?''
he asked.

"Again," Frate said, "I can only say not to my knowledge. That is, I had never seen them before. If you like,
though, I can ask around of some of the dealers, and the
girls. They may have seen them before."

"That would be very helpful."

"Of course."

"Was Walt with anyone at the time—uh, that you know
of?"

"Do you mean a woman?"

"I mean anyone, man or woman."

"Well," Frate said, "I believe there was a woman."

"Do you know who she was?"

Frate moved in his chair, perhaps the first sign that he
was uncomfortable.

"I believe I do."

"And was she a guest of the hotel?"

"Yes."

"What's her name?"

Frate frowned.

"I'll have to check on that."

"Is she still here?"

"I . . . believe so," Frate said. "I'd have to check to be
sure."

"Would you? Again, it would be very helpful."

"I'll see what I can do, Mr. Adams."

"I'd appreciate it. I'd be very interested in talking to
her."

"I'll have word sent to your room as soon as I know,"
Frate said.

"Thank you."

"Do you have any other questions?"

Clint asked a few more, but he'd found out what he
wanted to know. The hotel and the casino were nervous

about what had happened, were quick to deny any involvement, and were uncomfortable with questions regarding any companions Walt Gordon may have had while he was there.

Which led Clint to believe that the woman Gordon had been with was a prostitute—possibly employed by the hotel, which would make her a very high-priced prostitute.

FIFTEEN

Clint left Donald Frate's office and found his way back to the expansive hotel lobby. The Alhambra was possibly the fanciest of all the gaming hotels in Portsmouth Square, and it was certainly not the type of place Clint would have expected to find a man like Heck Thomas, but there he was, standing right smack-dab in the center of the lobby, looking out of place and lost.

Thomas actually seemed relieved when he saw Clint walking toward him.

"You, too, Heck?" he asked without preamble.

"If you're talkin' about what I think you're talkin' about, the answer's hell yeah."

Clint took the business card from his pocket and Heck Thomas produced its twin—or triplet, considering Bat had one, too.

"Anybody else we know?" Heck asked, returning the card to his pocket.

"Bat's here."

"Well, that's good," Heck said. "I wasn't sure I was going to be able to operate in this fancified environment. Having the two of you here should make it easier."

"Let's have a drink and talk about it."

"Okay," Heck said, "but not here, okay? Let's go someplace where I can be comfortable."

"Lead the way, then," Clint said.

A half hour later, when they both had a beer in front of them and were seated at a table in the Bucket of Blood Saloon on the Barbary Coast, Clint shook his head.

"I know I told you to lead the way, but—"

"Come on, you been down here before," Heck said.

"Many times," Clint said, "but what we want is in the Square. I thought you just wanted a place to have a drink and talk."

"I'm supposed to meet somebody down here in a couple of hours."

"About this?"

Heck Thomas nodded.

"Before I got on the train I sent a couple of telegrams to some contacts of mine."

That reminded Clint that he was supposed to send a telegram to Rick Hartman to let him know where he was staying. He still had some time to get that done today, before meeting Bat for dinner at seven.

"Okay," Heck said, "tell me your story and I'll tell you mine."

They each listened while the other one talked and then got two fresh beers.

"I'm impressed," Clint said.

"Don't be," the detective said. "They weren't that good, and I was lucky."

"You're being modest."

"What about you?"

"Mine were good, but I was better."

"No modesty there," Heck said, "which ain't like you at all, so I know you're kiddin'."

"What happened with your job for the railroad?"

"I turned it over to somebody else," Heck said. "Fellow named Foxx. When somebody's tryin' to kill me, that takes priority over any job."

"And do you know about the others?"

"I'm a detective, ain't I?" Heck asked. "Baker, Miller, and Gordon. Walt was the most recent one, so I came here."

"Did you know Gordon personally?"

"I knew him," Thomas said. "Didn't like him, but I knew him."

"What do you think is going on?"

"Well, since you and Bat are here—anybody other than you fellas?"

"Not that I've heard, but I'm still checking," Clint said.

"Well, with you fellas, me, and the other three it looks like somebody's got it in for fellas with reputations."

"You think the card represents some kind of organization?"

"Sure, don't you?"

"Well, yeah, but I've been told I'm paranoid."

"I'm not sure I know what that means, but if it means nuts, then you ain't, 'cause that's what I think, too."

"Who'd be at the head of something like that?"

"That's easy," Heck said. "Somebody with money."

"Hmm, I think you're right about that. What time's your meeting?"

"Seven."

"That's when I'm meeting with Bat to find out what he learned today," Clint said. "We'll all have to meet later on."

"How about here at ten tonight?" Heck asked.

"I don't know if I can drag Bat here."

"He's wearing them fancy clothes of his?"

"When isn't he? Do you know a place called the Golden Nickel? It's off the Square, but not by much."

"I know it."

"How about there?"

"That's fine with me. Are you and Masterson staying at the Alhambra?"

"We are."

"I'm payin' my own bills this trip, so I'm staying in a dive down here."

"I can probably get you a room at the Alhambra," Clint said. "I have the ear of the casino manager."

"That's okay," Heck said. "It'd be too rich for my blood, anyway. I'm not a gambler, and their food would probably be so good it would kill me."

"Suit yourself."

They talked a little while longer, and then got up and left together.

"My meeting's down the street," Heck said. "I'd invite you along, but my guy is a mite skittish."

"That's okay—unless you want me to watch your back for you."

"No, I'll be fine," the railroad detective said. "I fit in down here. You, on the other hand . . ."

"What about me?"

"Well, I don't see you fitting in here, or in the Square— or maybe I see you fitting in both places. How do you do that?"

"Beats me."

"That'd be a valuable talent for a detective."

"I'm not looking to be a detective," Clint said. "I'm just looking to find whoever's hiring guns to kill us off. It's as if we were a species that someone was trying to wipe out."

"I never thought of it that way before," Heck said, "but maybe we are."

SIXTEEN

Clint went back to the Alhambra, but he was half an hour early for his dinner meeting with Bat. He decided to go into the casino and take a look around. There was no time for poker, but maybe a hand of blackjack or a spin or two of the roulette wheel. It was early enough that his casual dress—not as plain as Heck Thomas but not as "fancified" as Bat Masterson—was good enough.

Even though it was early, there were plenty of people gambling, including some unaccompanied women. There was a time when that would have been unusual, or even not allowed, but times had changed, and women were changing with them—possibly even more than men were.

Several women gave him a couple of looks, and if he hadn't been killing time before meeting Bat there were one of two he might have talked to. At one point he wondered if any of these women was the one Walt Gordon had been with the night he died. If she was a high-priced prostitute, though, she probably didn't come out until the high rollers did.

He played a few hands of blackjack—which he lost—and played two spins of the roulette wheel, betting five dollars each time. He lost the first and won the second, so

by the time he left the casino to go to Delmonico's to meet
Bat he had broken even.

When Clint reached Delmonico's Bat was already seated
and had a beer in front of him. As Clint approached the
table Bat waved to a waiter, who quickly appeared at
Clint's elbow with a beer.

"Thank you."

"Steak?" Bat asked him.

"What else?"

Bat held up two fingers to the waiter, who nodded and
hurried off.

"What'd you find out?" Bat asked.

Clint gave Bat a brief rundown of his conversation with
Frate, and then told him about bumping into Heck Thomas.

"Thomas is a hell of a detective," Bat said. "Maybe
he's the one to sort this out. Or we could call in your buddy,
Talbot Roper."

"This is personal, Bat," Clint said. "I'm not going to
get Roper or anyone else involved. You, Heck, and me,
we're involved already."

"You're right," Bat said. "Well, I didn't find out much.
Gordon was not the kind of man who had many male
friends."

"Heck knew him but didn't like him."

"That's what I got. Not too many people are sorry he's
dead. I guess we're going to have to wait until we can meet
this woman he was with. You think she was a whore?"

"As uncomfortable as Frate was talking about her, that's
what I think."

"Sure," Bat said, "he wouldn't want anyone to know
that the casino—and the hotel—supplied their customers
with whores—like nobody knows, anyway."

"Knowing and proving are two different things."

The waiter arrived with their steaks just then, cooked to

perfection and garnished with several different vegetables.

"I've arranged for us to meet with Heck at the Golden Nickel later on."

"What's wrong with the Alhambra?"

"He feels out of his element there."

"If I remember correctly," Bat said, cutting into his steak, "we'd just need to get him some new clothes. Come to think of it"—he pointed with his knife—"you could use some new—"

"I've got something in my room that fits the Alhambra, thanks."

"Just trying to be helpful. Did you check the newspapers like you said?"

"Didn't have time," Clint replied. "I'll get to it tomorrow." Then he slapped his forehead with his hand.

"What is it?"

"I forgot to send Rick a telegram telling him where I was staying. He might have some information."

"Telegraph offices will be closed when we finish eating," Bat said, "but they might be able to help you at the hotel."

"That's right," Clint said, "they have their own wire, don't they?"

"They do," Bat said. "They want the high rollers to have the convenience of being able to wire their banks for more money."

"Smart practice. After dinner I'll go back there and see if they'll let me use it."

"This fella you saw today? It was Donald Frate, wasn't it?"

"That's right, it was."

"Real big fella?"

"That's him"

"Didn't mention me, did you?"

"Your name didn't come up."

"Well," Bat said, "if he's good at his job he knows who's staying in the hotel."

"He struck me as being good at what he does."

"That's what I've always heard."

They finished their dinner, topped it off with some pie, and then left together.

"I'm going back to the hotel. What about you?"

"I think I'll talk to some of the others," Bat said. "Be a shame to waste any of our time here."

"Maybe we should stick together, watch each other's backs."

Bat smiled at Clint.

"Who would try for us if we're together?" Bat said. "The next time somebody does try, I want to try and take him alive."

"You have a point," Clint said. "Just be real careful, okay?"

"Same to you. See you at ten at the Nickel."

Clint watched as Bat crossed the street and was swallowed up by the darkness, then he turned and walked toward the Alhambra.

SEVENTEEN

When Clint got back to the Alhambra he saw the head desk clerk, Harold, coming toward him.

"Mr. Adams," Harold said, "just the man I was looking for."

"What can I do for you, Harold?"

Harold blinked and said, "Well, nothing, sir. I was looking for you to do something for you."

"Which is?"

"Mr. Frate has found the woman you wanted to talk to. I'm to give you her name."

"Which is?"

"Deborah Whitcomb, sir."

"And is she a guest in the hotel?"

"She, uh, will probably be in the casino about now."

Clint noticed how Harold had avoided answering the question.

"And how will I recognize her?"

"Well, she's quite lovely, really, with black hair worn, you know, up," Harold used his hands to illustrate, "and, uh, she's wearing a red gown that's sort of, you know, sparkly." Again, his hands fluttered about.

"I see," Clint said. "Well, she shouldn't be too hard to

find. And has Mr. Frate told her that I want to talk to her?"

"Oh, yes, sir," Harold said. "She's, uh, prepared to talk to you."

"Well, this is good news, Harold," Clint said. "Thank you very much."

"Yes, sir," Harold said. "Anytime I can be of any service, just let me know."

"I'll do that, Harold," Clint said. "Thanks again."

"Oh, and would you tell Mr. Masterson the same thing?" Harold asked.

"Yes, I will."

"Thank you."

Clint left Harold standing there in the lobby with his hero worship and went to his room to dress for an evening of gambling.

Actually, the suit of clothes Clint had brought with him probably wasn't in Bat Masterson's league. Still, it was black, and he had a tie to wear, so it would do. He thought briefly about leaving his gun belt in the room and tucking his little Colt New Line into his belt, but decided against it. If someone was going to make another attempt on his life, he wanted to be well armed to ward it off.

Dressed for the evening he went back to the lobby and made his way to the casino. As he entered there was a set of steps before him, four of them leading down, but he remained where he was in order to survey the room. He saw three women wearing red, but had no difficulty picking out Deborah Whitcomb, as neither of the other two women filled out their dresses the way she filled out hers.

She was standing at one of the roulette tables, surrounded by men as she made her play. From where he stood he got a good view of her amazing cleavage as she leaned over to play her number. Her breasts were creamy and large, and threatened to spill out of her gown.

He went down the steps then, and negotiated his way through the crowd to the roulette table.

He arrived in time to hear her say, "Oh, pooh, I just missed that time."

Clint managed to squeeze his way through until he was standing next to her. Her perfume rushed into his nostrils, a heady scent that suited her. She was average height, but that was the only thing average about her.

"Try again," he said. "Maybe I'll bring you luck."

She turned her head to see who was speaking, and he was startled at how violet her eyes were.

"Do you really think so?"

"You never know unless you try. What's your number?" he asked.

"Fifteen," she said. "I always play fifteen."

"Allow me."

He bought some chips and then placed twenty dollars on number fifteen as the wheel started to turn and the man turning it said, "No more bets, please."

He and Deborah Whitcomb watched as the wheel went around and the white ball went around the opposite way. Finally, the ball dropped onto the wheel and began to bounce from number to number until it settled right on the number fifteen.

"Fifteen . . . the lady in red is a winner."

Deborah's eyes widened and she once again turned their light on him.

"You were right! You are lucky."

A tower of chips was pushed in front of her, over seven hundred dollars worth.

Clint leaned closer to her so that only she could hear what he had to say.

"I hope that will pay for a few moments of your time," he whispered. "I'm Clint Adams. I think Mr. Frate told you I'd be around."

She looked at him again and there was a change in her eyes. They were no longer wide and innocent, but slightly narrowed and shrewd.

"Are you saying I should walk away while I'm hot?" she asked.

"One turn of the wheel doesn't make you hot," he said. "If you think it does, just let it ride."

"All of it?"

"You'll need Frate's okay for that."

She made a face, looked at the croupier, and said, "Cash me in, please."

EIGHTEEN

"What did Frate tell you about me?" she asked when they were sitting in the bar—not the saloon, which was off to one side of the building, away from the casino, but a bar area that had been installed right in the casino. If this was Frate's idea, it was a good one, Clint thought. Gamblers often got thirsty and sometimes liked to take a break from the action, and this area afforded them the opportunity to satisfy both needs.

"Not much," Clint said. "Just that you were with Walt Gordon the night he was killed."

She studied him over the rim of her glass while she sipped her wine. His beer mug was on the table in front of him.

"Did he tell you what I . . . do?"

"He didn't tell me anything more than that," Clint said, "and I don't much care *why* you were with Walt or *what* you do for a living."

"But you know, don't you?"

"I have a pretty good idea, Miss Whitcomb."

"You're very polite."

"Always, to a lady."

She put her glass down.

"Well, you certainly have paid for the right," she said, "so ask me what you want to ask me."

"Was that the first night you were with Walt?"

"No," she said, "the second."

"Had you—" he started, then stopped short.

"I'll make it easy on you, Mr. Adams," she said. "Apparently, Walt came to San Francisco with money burning a hole in his pocket. He wanted to gamble it or spend it . . . on me."

"You specifically?"

"I had been . . . recommended to him. So he paid me for two nights and a day. We'd already had the first night; he was killed before we could have the second. Are you here looking for a refund?"

"No," he said, "not at all. I'm here looking for whoever had Walt Gordon killed."

"Somebody *had* him killed? I just thought it was the same stupid fight men are always having."

"Not in this instance."

"And what's your interest? Were you friends?"

"Acquaintances," Clint said, "but apparently the same person or persons who had him killed is trying to have me killed."

"Really? Is that the truth?"

"It is," he said. "And it's not only me. Two others were killed, and they tried for two more."

"All friends of yours?"

"The dead ones were . . . colleagues, but the other two who survived are friends. Maybe you've heard of them? Heck Thomas?"

"Can't say I have."

"Bat Masterson?"

Her eyes widened.

"Well, of course I've heard of him, and of you. This Heck . . ."

"He's a detective," Clint said, "and also very good with a gun."

"Let me get this straight," she said, sitting forward so that her cleavage tantalized him—and she knew it. "Someone is trying to kill famous gunmen?"

"It seems that way."

"Or is someone a little . . . paranoid?"

"Whichever it is," Clint said, picking up his beer, "I'm going to find out."

"And this Heck and Bat Masterson are also in town to find out?"

"Yes."

"That makes you a formidable trio—but will three be enough?"

"I don't know," he said. "We don't know what we're up against yet."

"And you think I can help?"

"You were with Walt all that day and evening?"

She nodded. "Up until that man picked a fight with him and he went outside."

"Did he speak to anyone else that day?"

"No harsh words, if that's what you mean."

"And the man who picked the fight, had you seen him before?"

"No."

"And the other men involved?"

"I didn't see them at all," she said. "You see, I didn't go outside. That sort of thing doesn't do anything for me."

Clint swirled what beer was left in his mug and stared into it.

"Any more questions?" she asked.

"I'm thinking."

"Time is money for me, you know."

He looked at her.

"I think I bought a little more than an hour."

"Touché," she said. "You did, indeed. By the way, how did you know I'd hit if I played again?"

"I didn't."

"But you put twenty dollars on the number."

"I was feeling lucky."

"Maybe you'd like to come back to the wheel with me?" she asked.

"No, thanks, but I'm sure there are a lot of fellas over there waiting for you."

"Perhaps you're right," she said, "but none of them can afford me."

"What makes you think I can?"

"Just a hunch. What about the rest of those questions?" she asked.

"Maybe you should go and I'll spend some time thinking of some."

"Fine," she said, putting her glass down and pushing her chair back. "You have a credit with me. Cash it in . . . anytime."

Her inflection and the look she gave him made her point very obvious.

"I will."

She smiled and said, "A pleasure to meet you, Mr. Adams. Maybe you could bring your friend Mr. Masterson around later on, or tomorrow."

"I thought gunmen didn't do anything for you."

"They don't," she said, "but *gamblers* . . . that's something else again!"

NINETEEN

Clint remained where he was and had another beer before leaving and heading for the Golden Nickel. The Nickel was more like a saloon and gambling hall from Tombstone or Dodge. It was as if someone had lifted it from there and dropped it here. He walked in and felt as if he hadn't left Rick's Place in Labyrinth. In fact, this was the kind of place Rick would open if he moved to San Francisco.

Once again he was reminded that he was to have sent a telegram to Rick in Labyrinth. What was wrong with him? He'd have to talk with Harold when he got back to the Alhambra, if the man was still on duty.

He had arrived before Heck or Bat so he got himself a beer from the bar and went to a back table. The place was crowded, but most of the men and women present were standing at one gaming table or another, so getting a desired table was no problem. "Desired" meant one where he could sit with his back to the wall and observe the entire room.

Heck arrived before Bat, saw Clint, and got himself a beer before joining him.

"Find out anything?" Clint asked.

"Something, maybe," Heck said. "One of my contacts

73

says he heard about someone who was hiring guns for a special project.''

''Project?''

''That's the word he used.''

''And?''

''And he went for . . . well, an interview, I guess you'd call it, but he wasn't good enough.''

''So they turned him down?''

''Right.''

''Can he tell you who was hiring?''

''No,'' Heck said. ''He can't even tell me where to go to check it out. He says he went back to the same place, but it was empty.''

''Okay,'' Clint said, ''so now we know that somebody was hiring guns.''

''But why didn't they try to hire the best?'' Heck asked. ''Why not you? Wyatt? Bat? One of us?''

''We still haven't heard from everybody,'' Clint said, ''but now instead of asking everyone if an attempt has been made to kill them, we'll have to ask if an attempt has been made to hire them.''

At that point Bat entered and took the same route to the table, stopping first for a beer. He and Heck shook hands, and then he was told what Heck had found out.

''What about you?'' Bat asked Clint.

''I spoke with the woman,'' Clint said. ''She's a high-priced prostitute who works the high rollers.''

''What was she doing with Walt?'' Heck asked.

''She says he came to San Francisco with money to burn.''

''And where would he have gotten that?'' Bat asked.

Clint shrugged.

''What's this lady look like?''

''She's beautiful,'' Clint said. ''There's no other way to describe her. Oh, and she wants to meet you, Bat.''

"Really?" Bat asked. "You mean there's a woman who's met you and she wants to meet me? Are you losing your touch, Clint?"

Clint laughed.

"Apparently reputations with a gun don't impress her, but reputations as a gambler do."

"Bat has both," Heck said.

Bat simply inclined his head, as if bowing.

"So what do we do now?" Heck asked.

"I'm going to send a telegram to Rick Hartman tomorrow and see what he's found out. I'll also send one each to the people I contacted before. Let's see if we can find out who they tried to hire."

"What if they tried to hire Baker, Miller, and Walt Gordon?" Bat asked. "And what if they refused, so they were killed first?"

"Wait a minute," Heck said. "I've got another question. What if Walt *was* hired? That's where he got the money to burn."

"So why'd they kill him?" Bat asked.

"Maybe he didn't perform as he was supposed to," Clint said.

"You mean he just took their money but didn't do the job?"

Clint nodded.

"Well, that makes some kind of sense," Bat said. "But how can we find out about the others? Baker and Miller?"

"Do we know if they had any family?" Clint asked.

"I don't know anything about them," Bat said.

"Me, neither," Heck chimed in.

"Well, we know they didn't try to hire any of us, right?"

"No," Bat said.

"I think I'd remember," Thomas said.

"And not me," Clint said. "I guess there's nothing to do except wait until tomorrow. I'll find out something from

Rick, and I'll take a look at the newspapers."

"There are still one or two people I can talk to," Heck said. "What are you going to do, Bat?"

"You heard what Clint said," Bat replied. "There's a beautiful lady who wants to meet me."

TWENTY

When Clint and Bat got back to the Alhambra, Bat decided to do some gambling. As always, he was dressed for it. His evening wear would have fit in in New York or even London.

"What are you going to do?" he asked Clint.

"I want to see about sending those telegrams tomorrow," he said. "It would save me time—and possibly money—if I could do it here from the hotel."

"Don't forget you have a lady to introduce me to," Bat said.

"I described her to you," Clint said. "She won't be hard to find. Look for the table where all the men are huddled."

"Nothing doin'," Bat said. "I don't want to deprive you of making this introduction."

"I'll be along, then," Clint said. "Try not to take the casino for all they're worth the first night."

"I'll play with caution," Bat said, "but only for a while. Besides, there are other places in town to gamble after I've bankrupted this place."

They split up and Clint went to the front desk.

"Can I help you?" the desk clerk—who was not Harold—asked.

"Yes, I'm looking for Harold."

"Oh, Harold left for the day, sir. Are you a guest of the hotel?"

"Yes, I am. My name is Clint Adams."

"Oh, yes, of course, Mr. Adams," the man said. "We have instructions to make your stay as pleasant as possible."

"You do?"

"Yes, sir."

"From who?"

"From our Mr. Frate, sir."

Clint wondered how many people Frate belonged to.

"My name is Louis, sir. What can I do for you?"

"Well, Louis, I was wondering if the hotel had a telegraph line."

"Well, sir, it's not really the hotel, but the casino that has one. They reserve its use for high rollers, if you get my meaning."

"I get your meaning, Louis, now see if you get mine. I'd like to use the telegraph line tomorrow morning, and since it belongs to the casino, and Mr. Frate has already told you to give me what I want, I guess there won't be a problem with that, will there?"

"Well, sir, I suppose there won't."

"Good, then maybe you can make the arrangements for me. I'll be down here tomorrow at eight a.m."

"Eight a.m., yes, sir," Louis said. "I'll talk to Mr. Frate and we'll have the telegraph operator here waiting for you as soon as, uh, Mr. Frate approves it."

"Good," Clint said. "Thanks for your help, Louis."

"Yes, sir, no problem."

"And would you do one more thing for me?"

"What's that?"

"Would you let Harold know I'd like to see him when he comes in?"

"Yes, sir, I'll do that, too."

"Good."

"Are you going to your room now, sir?"

"No," Clint said, "I'm going to go in and do some gambling for a while."

"All right, sir," Louis said. "Good luck to you."

"Thanks."

Louis seemed real nervous, as if he'd promised something he couldn't deliver. Still, Clint was sure—well, almost sure—that when he told Frate what Clint wanted the casino manager would okay it.

Clint decided to spend the rest of the night trying to take some money out of the casino operation that "everybody's" Mr. Frate was the manager of.

TWENTY-ONE

The first thing Clint saw when he entered the casino was Deborah's red dress, surrounded by men. He looked around but couldn't spot Bat at that moment. He stepped down and began to walk leisurely around, looking for a likely place to play.

There were a few house-dealt poker games going on, but there were no empty chairs. Likewise the blackjack tables were all full. He could have made it to a roulette wheel, but felt he might have exhausted all his luck earlier in the evening. Faro was available, but although he'd dealt it in his time, he didn't like to play it.

The Alhambra was busy, and it looked like if he wanted to gamble it would have to be someplace else.

He'd managed to locate Bat, though. Apparently he'd gotten the last seat at one of the blackjack tables. Clint knew that Bat played blackjack for fun. When he wanted to play for money he played poker, but he didn't play house bet games. He only played in private games.

"Can't find a seat?"

Clint turned and saw Donald Frate approaching. He'd forgotten how big the man was.

"Looks like a busy night."

81

"It's like this most every night," Frate said, stopping next to him.

"Are you looking for me?"

"Not really," Frate said, "although I have heard about your request for tomorrow."

"And?"

Frate pursed his lips for a moment then said, "We usually reserve that service for high rollers."

"I realize that."

For a few moments of silence Frate's eyes moved around the room, noticing everything. Finally, he looked at Clint.

"It shouldn't be a problem. I'll have an operator for you at eight a.m."

"Thanks," Clint said. "I appreciate it."

"Did you manage to speak with Miss Whitcomb?"

"I did."

"And?"

"She was very helpful."

"Good," Frate said. "I told her I'd appreciate it if she was . . . cooperative."

"And she was."

"I noticed your friend has found a chair at a blackjack table."

"He's just whiling away the time."

"You know," Frate said, "if you and he were interested in a private game, I could arrange it."

"Not what we're here for."

"What would he say?"

"Bat would probably say yes."

"I won't ask him, though," Frate said. "I'll leave that to you, if you want to tell him."

"Thanks."

"Can I buy you a drink?"

"I don't think so," Clint said. "I might go out and get some air."

"Check the competition?"

"Maybe," Clint said.

"I don't blame you," Frate said. "You usually have to get here earlier in the night and stake out your territory."

"I can see that."

"Of course," Frate said, "there always seems to be room at one of the roulette tables."

"Roulette's not my game."

"Why not?"

"Too much luck involved."

"I heard you had some luck earlier."

"You heard wrong," Clint said. "That was Miss Whitcomb's number. The luck was hers."

"Ah."

Which meant that Frate already knew that Clint had talked to Deborah Whitcomb before he asked.

"Good luck to you," Frate said. "Everything will be ready for you come morning."

"Thank you, Mr. Frate."

"Just Frate will do," the man said, and moved off to be swallowed up by the crowd.

Clint was making his mind up about what to do when Deborah Whitcomb appeared.

"Is your friend here?" she asked.

"Bat? He's playing blackjack."

"I thought poker was his game."

"It is," Clint said. "He's just killing time. Would you like to meet him now?"

"I don't think so," she said. She looked around, then looked back at him. "It's a slow night."

"The place is packed."

She smiled.

"Slow for me."

"Oh."

"I thought maybe . . ." she said, raising her elegant eyebrows.

"Sorry," he said. "I don't pay for sex."

She laughed, a deep, throaty sound, an honest laugh as if she found him very amusing.

"I didn't ask you to," she said, "now did I?"

Clint decided not to tell Bat where he was going. It would only disappoint him.

TWENTY-TWO

On the way up to his room Clint said, "I thought you said you wanted to meet Bat."

"I do," she said, "but later. I thought you might have some more questions to ask me . . . after."

"I might," he said, "after . . ."

In his room she turned into his arms and they kissed. It was a kiss that went on for a long time because they were both immediately comfortable with it. So comfortable, in fact, that it seemed to make her nervous and, after a few moments—or minutes—she pulled away, putting her hand against his chest.

"What is it?"

"Give me a minute," she said, moving away from him.

"Did I do something wrong?"

"Wrong? No, no, there's nothing wrong. In fact, it's too right."

She put one hand on her hip and the other to her forehead.

"Deborah—"

"Mmmm, wait a minute," she said, holding her hand out to him. "All my life I've been able to kiss a man and not feel anything. It's important to my profession, do you know what I mean?"

"I would think so," he said, "but you're forgetting one thing."

"What?"

"You're not here professionally." He walked over to her and put his hands on her bare upper arms. He looked down at her beautiful face, her full, deep cleavage. "You're here because you want to be. You're *supposed* to feel something under these circumstances."

"I am?"

"Yes."

She looked up at him and said, "Then I guess I'm doing it right, too, aren't I?"

"You're doing it very right."

He pulled her to him and kissed her again. She moaned, leaned against him, and opened her mouth to him.

During the kiss he began to undo her dress and she let him. In the end she allowed him to undress her completely, which he did with great pleasure. When she was naked he stepped back and looked at her. Her body was lush and full, with heavy breasts and broad hips, full thighs, and an almost plump butt. He thought, in that moment, that he couldn't have asked for a more perfect woman to take to bed.

"Now you," she said.

He undressed for her, taking his time. She was a high-priced prostitute who was, apparently, on vacation for this night, for it was he who was in control.

"I think," she said slowly, looking him up and down, "I'm just going to enjoy myself tonight."

"I know you will," he said. "Come on, come to bed."

He took her hand and led her to the bed. She lay down on it and he sat next to her.

"Aren't you going to lie down?" she asked.

"After a while," he said. "First I want to look at you, but I'm going to use my hands as well as my eyes. Is that all right?"

"That's fine," she said. "Why do I get the feeling that you've been with more than a few women?"

"I've had my share," he said. "Just relax. I'm going to turn the light down."

He got up, turned the flame on the wall gas lamp down low, then returned to the bed. The low light gave her skin a glow. He ran the palm of his hand over her breasts, lightly rubbing the nipples until she licked her lips and moaned. He leaned on one arm next to her and began to kiss and lick her breasts while sliding his other hand down between her legs. He found her hot and wet, and slid his fingers along her moist slit while continuing to work on her nipples with his mouth, tongue, and teeth.

"Oooh, God," she said, squirming, catching her breath, reaching for his head with her hands and holding him to her breasts.

"Mmmm," she said, "that feels so good."

He moved his lips from her breasts to her ribs, and her belly, probing her navel with his tongue and then continuing on down until his tongue was tracing a wet path through her pubic hair, which was just as black as the hair on her head.

Finally, he moved his fingers and tasted her sweetness with his tongue. This caused her to catch her breath again and lift her hips off the bed. He allowed the pressure of his tongue to become heavier, began to taste her in long, loving licks that had her panting and reaching for him.

"Oh, my . . . I'm not used to such . . . treatment from a man. . . ."

"You should get used to it," he said, kissing her inner thighs. The skin there was like silk. He slid his hands beneath her to cup her full buttocks and then began to work on her in earnest with his mouth, probing and licking with his tongue, nipping and teasing with his teeth until her breath was coming heavily.

"God . . ." she gasped, "you're not going to . . . you can't make me . . . I haven't . . . ooooh, yesssss . . ."

Her belly began to tremble and then her entire body was wracked with waves of passion that took her breath away. She bucked beneath him as he fought to keep his mouth on her. He stayed with her until she settled down, no longer writhing but still breathing hard, both hands over her eyes as she fought to catch her breath.

"God," she said finally, "it's been so *long* since I felt anything like that . . . no, actually . . . I've *never* felt anything like that before."

"Good."

"I thought I was going to *die!*"

"No," he said, moving up alongside her again, "you're going to live through this night, Deborah."

She looked at him, then down at his penis, which was rigid and so red it was almost purple.

"You didn't finish," she said. "Don't you want to? I can use my mouth, or you can—"

"Relax," he said, putting his hand on her belly and just rubbing in slow, soothing circles, "there's no hurry. We have all night . . . unless you have someplace else to go?"

"No," she said, "I have no place else to go. I've just never known a man to put his pleasure second before."

"Don't worry," he said, kissing her shoulder, then her neck, causing her to moan again, "there's plenty of pleasure to go around."

TWENTY-THREE

She woke him during the night and whispered in his ear, "It's time."

"For what?" he asked, trying to take her in his arms, but she pushed away from him.

"It's time for me to show you what I'm very good at."

"You've already shown me that," he said.

"No," she said, kissing his belly, his thighs, "I've shown you how well I can take pleasure. Now I will show you how well I can give it."

"Deborah—" He stopped short when she slid her hand beneath his testicles and fondled them gently. She continued to kiss his thighs, his belly, planting kisses all around his penis, everywhere but right on it, which—after a while—started to drive him crazy.

"For God's sake—" he said.

"What?" she asked sweetly, innocently.

"Stop teasing me."

"Oh," she said, sliding her fingers around his stiff penis, "that's all part of the pleasure. You'll see."

Now she slid her fingers up and down his shaft with one hand while continuing to fondle his balls with the other. Every so often she leaned over and gave the head of his penis a lick, then tickled the spot just beneath the head with the tip of her tongue.

"Deborah . . ." he said tightly.

"Shhh," she said, right against him, "it's coming, don't worry."

She released him then and placed both of her hands on top of his thighs, then she swooped down with her head and captured him in her hot mouth. She moaned as she took the length of him all the way in, a moan he felt, and then her head began to move up and down, her mouth began to slide up and down on him, wetly, avidly, sucking gently at first and then more insistently.

She moved her hands again, touching him gently but firmly, easily but insistently, sliding her fingertips over tender parts of him while she continued to suck. At one point she released him from her mouth only to recapture him, this time between her full breasts, and then she moved so that he was fucking her between her breasts, and as the head of his penis peeked out from her cleavage she would swipe at it with her tongue until finally she took him in her mouth again and this time there was no doubt about what she was going to do. She held on to him with one hand around the base of him as her mouth sucked him, fucked him, and finally yanked his ejaculation from him. He exploded into her mouth and she drank of him greedily, like a cat with milk, and when he was finished she licked him clean before moving up to lie on him, her breasts pressed firmly to his chest, her hands reaching between them.

"You're still hard," she said, sounding amazed.

"Yes."

"Good." She adjusted herself to that fact quickly, lifted her hips, and took him into the wet steamy depths of her. She rode him that way for a long time, for although he was hard it would take him a while before he was ready to explode again. By the time he was they were both sweating and grunting and lurching at each other, and when he did ejaculate again she brought herself down on him tightly and began to grind on him, back and forth, back and forth, growling as he filled her, raking his chest with her nails and then falling on him, her mouth seeking his, sucking his tongue in greedily, rubbing the plush curves of her body against him, enjoying the way his chest hair felt on her nipples. She took her weight on her hands, then, so that her breasts were dangling in his face, and he took one and then the other in his mouth, sucking and biting her nipples again and again, alternating, all the while still inside of her, and then, amazingly, beginning to swell again. . . .

Her eyes widened and she asked happily, "Again?"

He laughed and said, "If I don't die of a heart attack first."

"Oh," she said, "I don't think I'm going to allow that."

TWENTY-FOUR

He left her asleep in his bed the next morning and went down to the lobby, presenting himself at the front desk by 8:05. Harold was the clerk on duty and he smiled as he greeted Clint.

"Mr. Adams. So nice to see you this morning."

"Good morning, Harold."

"Everything is ready for you," Harold said. "If you give me a moment to get someone to relieve me, I'll take you over there."

Clint didn't know where "there" was, but he nodded and said, "Of course."

It only took a moment for Harold to get a younger man to stand in for him, and then he was at Clint's side.

"Will you follow me?"

"Sure."

As he led Clint down a hallway, he said, "I understand you wanted to see me today."

"Yes, if you have some time," Clint said. "I get the feeling you know more about what's going on around here than anyone. Am I right?"

"Well," Harold said modestly, "I do manage to keep my ear to the ground."

"That's what I thought," Clint said. "What about at lunchtime? Could we go someplace and talk? I'll make it worth your while."

"I think that can be arranged, sir," Harold said, "but, if you don't mind, it would be better if we met someplace outside the hotel."

"You name it."

Harold thought a moment then named a café and gave Clint directions to get there.

"Is twelve-thirty all right?" Harold asked.

"That's fine. I appreciate this, Harold."

"No trouble at all," the head desk clerk said, "happy to oblige. Here we are, the telegraph room."

Harold opened the door, took Clint inside, and introduced him to the key operator, whose name was Buzz. Clint wondered about the origin of the name—whether it was as obvious as it sounded—but didn't ask.

"Take good care of him, Buzz," Harold said. "He's a valued guest."

"No problem," Buzz said. "I got my instructions right from Mr. Frate."

"Mr. Adams?" Harold said. "Until later?"

"Thank you again, Harold."

"Think nothing of it, sir. All part of the service."

Harold left the room, and Clint turned to face the key operator. Buzz seemed an odd name for a man in his forties, but there it was.

"What can I do for you, sir?" Buzz asked.

"I'd like to write a number of messages for you to send, possibly as many as a dozen. Can you handle that?"

"I'm the best key operator in San Francisco, sir," Buzz said. "I can do anything."

"I intend to pay you for your time."

"Mr. Frate told me not to accept any money from you, sir," Buzz said.

"Well," Clint said, "what Mr. Frate doesn't know won't hurt him, eh?"

"Sir—"

"We'll talk about it when we're done, Buzz," Clint said. "Right now I'd like to start writing."

"Yes, sir," Buzz said, supplying pencil and paper, "here ya go. . . ."

By the time they finished Clint's hand was sore from writing, so he wondered how Buzz's hand was from operating the key.

"If any replies come in, just leave them at the desk for me."

"Yes, sir."

Clint took some money out and pressed it into Buzz's hand.

"This is between you and me," he said.

"Yes, sir," Buzz said, closing his hand around the bills, "thank you, sir."

"Thank you, Buzz."

Clint went out into the hallway and found his way back down the hall. When he got to the lobby he found Bat Masterson waiting there.

"Desk clerk told me what you were doing," Bat said. "I thought I'd wait for you for breakfast."

"I'm glad you did."

They started walking toward the hotel dining room.

"What happened to you last night?" Bat asked. "I thought you were going to introduce me to the lady?"

"I was going to," Clint said, unable to hide a smile, "but the lady had other plans."

Bat glanced at him quickly, assumed an insincere hurt look, and said, "You cad."

"Hey," Clint said, "it was her idea."

"I'm sure it was," Bat said. "Just for that I'm making you pay for breakfast."

TWENTY-FIVE

"I have a message for you from Mr. Frate," Clint said, when they had been seated and put in their orders for breakfast.

"You mean you did talk about me?"

"Not until last night," Clint said.

"What did he have to say?"

"He said he could set up a private game if we—if you— wanted him to."

"Hmmm," Bat said, "any game Frate sets up would be a big one. What did you tell him?"

"I told him I didn't come here to play poker."

Bat frowned.

"Well, neither did I, but a big game is a big game, Clint," he said. "Besides, where would we be safer but in a room full of poker players?"

"Bat," Clint said, "you can play if you want to. You don't have to justify it to me."

"I know, I know . . . tell me, did you get off all the telegrams you wanted to?"

"Yes, now we just have to wait for replies."

"What if they've struck again?" Bat asked. "Someplace else, far from here? Do we go there?"

"No," Clint said, "I have a hunch about that."

"Oh, good," Bat said, "I'm just in the mood to hear about hunches."

"I think an organization like this—"

"That's if we assume there is an organization," Bat interrupted.

"If we assume there is, I believe it would have to be run from here."

"Why here? Why not New York?"

"Too far from the West," Clint said.

"Why not Sacramento? Or Los Angeles?" Bat asked.

"That's what I mean," Clint said. "I think it's being run from this coast. But if I was going to pick a city, I'd say it's here."

"Why?"

"Because a lot of money is involved. They hired men to kill you, me, Heck, the three dead men—that's a big payroll."

"Okay," Bat said, "let's say you're right. What do we do now?"

"Now," Clint said, as the waiter appeared with their food, "we find them, and we find out what the hell this Circle-Nine means on the card."

"You make it sound so simple."

Clint looked up at the doorway to the dining room just as Heck Thomas walked in.

"There's Heck," he said and waved.

The railroad detective came over and sat down. Clint poured him a cup of coffee.

"I had a feeling you two would be up early," he said.

"You're going to have to let me help you pick out some clothes, Heck."

Heck smiled and said, "My clothes are fine, Bat. I'd never be able to wear one of those getups of yours."

Bat looked down at his suit and said, "Getup?"

"No offense," Thomas said. "They're just a little fancy for me."

"No offense taken," Bat said, although he didn't sound too convincing.

Clint ran down for Heck Thomas what he and Bat had just been discussing. While he was doing that the waiter came over and Heck ordered what Bat and Clint had, steak and eggs.

"I'll go along with that," Heck said when Clint was done, "but I still think some of the answers will be found where the money isn't, not where the money is."

"That'll be your job, then, Heck," Clint said. "You look low, and we'll look high."

"It's a deal," Thomas said. "I have to deal with enough money men when I work for the railroads."

"Clint."

Clint looked at Bat.

"What?"

"High stakes."

"What?"

"High stakes," Bat said again.

"That's what we're playing for, Bat," Clint said. "Our lives."

"No, you don't understand," Bat said.

"Explain it to me, then."

"The men behind this have money, we've agreed on that. Right?"

"Right."

"And we've agreed that some of them must be based here."

"Right again."

"Then some of them must be gamblers."

Clint stared at Bat, then said, "I see your point."

"I don't," Thomas said. "Somebody explain it to me."

"Bat's been offered a high-stakes poker game."

"At a time like this?"

"It's the perfect time," Bat said.

"How so?"

"If word gets out that Bat Masterson is looking for a game . . ." Clint said.

"Ah, I see," Thomas said. "Bat would be the bait."

"And say that three times fast," Bat said.

"What?"

Bat frowned at Heck Thomas, who he had always suspected had no sense of humor.

"Never mind. What do you think, Clint?"

"I think if you want to be bait that's up to you," Clint said, "and if you can make some money while you're at it, so much the better."

"You think someone who's already hired somebody to try to kill you would actually have the nerve to show up and play poker at the same table as you?" Thomas asked.

"I think it's a safe bet," Bat said, "that if I'm at a table of eight or nine men, at least one of them will be part of the inner circle of this."

Bat pulled out the business card with the Circle-Nine on it and placed it on the table.

"Wait a minute," Clint said, tapping the card. "You just said it."

"Said what?" Bat asked.

"Inner circle."

"So?"

"Don't you see?" Clint said. "That's what this could mean."

"Enlighten me," Bat said.

"Me, too," said Heck Thomas.

"This," Clint said, tapping the card again, "could mean 'Circle of Nine.' "

"Meaning we're looking for nine men?" Thomas asked.

"Nine men who came up with this plan," Bat said, "and are rich enough to finance it."

"Money men," Thomas said, shaking his head, "again."

TWENTY-SIX

Now Clint and Heck Thomas took the Circle-Nine cards from their pockets and put them on the table.

"Somebody's got to know something," Clint said.

"You're checking the newspapers today, right?" Thomas asked.

"That's right."

"I still have some contacts to make," Thomas said, and looked at Bat.

"I think I should talk to Frate about a poker game," Bat said, "but I'll tell him I want it truly to be high stakes, no pikers."

"He'll spread the word," Clint said, "and, hopefully, the right people will hear it."

"Which means somebody might even try to kill Bat before the game starts," Heck Thomas said.

"One of us is going to have to keep an eye on him at all times, once he talks to Frate," Clint said.

"We'll take shifts," Thomas said.

"And while we're doing that, the other will still have to poke around."

"But while we're watching Bat's back," Heck Thomas asked, "who's watching ours?"

"We'll just have to stay alert and be real careful," Clint said. "The one thing we do know from all of this is that this Circle-Nine, or Circle of Nine, is not ambushing anyone. They're basically calling us out, with the odds tipped in their favor."

"They want it to *look* like a fair fight," Bat said. "Why is that?"

"Nobody likes a back-shooter," Clint said, "and apparently they're trying to make a point."

"But . . . what?" Thomas asked.

"That's what we'll have to ask them, when we find them."

The waiter arrived with Heck's breakfast at that point, and at the same moment the head desk clerk, Harold, entered the dining room. He looked around, spotted them, and came walking over, digging into his pocket.

"Mr. Adams, a reply to one of your telegrams came in. I thought it might be important." He handed Clint the telegram.

"Thank you, Harold."

"Of course, sir," Harold said. "Enjoy the rest of your meal, gentlemen."

As Harold walked away, Bat said, "Helpful little cuss, ain't he?"

"I'm hoping he'll be even more helpful," Clint said. "I'll be talking to him again at lunchtime."

"Why?" Bat asked.

"Because I think he knows everything there is to know about what goes on at the Alhambra."

Clint unfolded the telegram and read it.

"What is it?" Bat asked.

"Who's it from?" Thomas asked.

"It's from Rick Hartman," Clint said. "Two more men have been killed."

"Damn!" Thomas said.

"Who?" Bat asked.

"And when?" Thomas added.

"After Gordon," Clint said. "Jeff Price, in New Orleans, and Baily Spenser, in Sacramento."

"I know both names," Bat said, "but not the men."

"I met Spenser once," Thomas said.

"Apparently," Clint said, lowering the telegram and looking at them, "there was also an attempt on Doc Holliday."

"Doc?" Bat asked. "Why bother? Doc's dying, anyway, poor bastard."

"That may be so," Clint said, "but if I know Doc he won't appreciate being rushed."

"Wonder what Doc will do?" Bat asked.

"Rick's already answered that," Clint said. "Doc's on his way here."

"Well," Thomas said, "with four of us here, at least we'll have someone to watch all of our backs."

Clint nodded and picked up his coffee. He knew that the last time he saw Doc his disease had been progressing. Would Doc Holliday be in any condition to help them when he arrived?

TWENTY-SEVEN

After breakfast they all walked out to the lobby together but separated from there.

"We didn't have a chance to talk about Miss Red Dress," Bat said. "You'll have to fill me in later."

"A gentleman doesn't kiss and tell, Bat."

"I know," Bat said, "that's why I'm counting on you to fill me in later."

Clint was walking past the front desk when Harold called him over.

"You received some more replies, Mr. Adams," he said, holding them out.

There were half a dozen. Clint read them right there in the lobby. Frank Leslie, Ben Thompson, Bass Reaves, Luke Short, and Fred Hammer had all been alerted to watch their backs. All reported that no one had tried for them yet and that they appreciated the warning. They also offered their help to Clint, if he needed it.

The sixth telegram was from Doc Holliday, who said he'd be arriving on the seven p.m. train . . . today! He said he'd appreciate being met so he didn't take a couple of bullets stepping off the train.

Clint folded all the telegrams and put them in his pocket.

He left for the newspaper office wondering if Doc would know anything about Wyatt Earp's whereabouts.

Clint spent time in the morgue of *The San Francisco Chronicle* reading up on the killings of Baker, Miller, and Gordon. He also searched for similar stories which may have not already been connected to the death of those three men. In addition, he looked for stories of shoot-outs that did not result in the deaths of a "famous" shootist. There were none that he could see, and the *Chronicle,* being a major newspaper, picked up almost every newsworthy story from around the country.

From this Clint concluded that this "Circle of Nine" had only begun operating within the past month. In fact, checking the dates of all the incidents, he figured he had been second or third on the list, with Bat coming after him. Obviously, whoever made the list had used some other criteria for the order than talent.

By the time he finished up in the morgue he was covered with dust, his hands were black from ink, and it was time to go meet with Harold, the head desk clerk.

When Clint reached the café, Harold was already sitting there with a pot of coffee and two cups.

"Sorry I'm late," Clint said, seating himself. "I was at the *Chronicle* going through their back issues."

"I have thought, since you and Mr. Masterson arrived, that something was going on," Harold said excitedly. "Am I about to be asked to help?"

"Well, Harold," Clint said, "that's exactly what I'm going to do."

"Wonderful!"

"But first we're going to order lunch."

• • •

Over lunch Clint pumped Harold for everything he could tell him about Walt Gordon's stay at the Alhambra.

"Did anyone ever come in and ask if he was registered?" he asked.

"Not to my knowledge," Harold said, "but I can ask some of the other desk clerks."

"Good. That would help. I'll need descriptions of anyone who asked."

"All right."

"Did you often see Mr. Gordon in the lobby?"

"In the lobby, yes, usually on his way to the casino."

"Alone?"

"Sometimes with Miss Whitcomb."

"Did you ever notice that he was being followed?"

Harold frowned, trying to remember.

"No."

Clint took the Circle-Nine business card from his pocket and put it on the table. Immediately, he sensed a change in Harold.

"Do you know what this is?"

"No."

"Have you ever seen it before? Or one like it?"

"No."

"Harold—"

"I'm sorry, Mr. Adams," Harold said, almost leaping from his chair. "It's getting late, and I have to get back to work."

"Okay," Clint said, "but we'll talk again, soon."

"Yes," Harold said, "soon," and he fled from the café.

Clint would have liked to talk with Harold some more, but he still had to go to some of the other newspaper offices.

He picked up the Circle-Nine card and put it back in his pocket. They would definitely talk again, later.

TWENTY-EIGHT

At five minutes to seven Clint stood on the platform waiting for the train to pull in. He had checked the station carefully, and now looked up and down the platform. There was no one in sight who looked as if he would pose a threat. Certainly, no single gunman would have been sent to dispatch Doc Holliday, so he was looking for two or—more likely—three men together. There were no such groups.

Finally he heard the train whistle, and then it appeared in the distance. He positioned himself so that he'd be right in the center of the train when it stopped, since he didn't know what car Doc would be getting off.

When the train stopped he kept busy, head swiveling, looking for Doc and on the lookout for trouble. The first appeared, the second never did.

Doc happened to get off the train near the center, and Clint spotted him immediately. Even as he approached the man, Doc was coughing into a handkerchief. When he saw Clint he seemed to get the coughing fit under control and tucked the colorful handkerchief away. He was carrying one bag, which he had set down in order to cough. Not to do so would have meant both hands were occupied, and

Clint knew what a negative that was to anyone who lived by the gun.

When Doc saw Clint he waited to shake hands, rather than pick up the bag and approach.

"Doc."

"Adams."

To say that they were friends would have been stretching a point. In truth, both counted Wyatt Earp among their closest and dearest friends, but they had never had much liking for each other. Respect, however, was another matter, and it existed between them in abundance.

So they shook hands respectfully, and then Doc picked up his bag.

"That all you got?" Clint asked.

"That's it."

"Come this way, then," Clint said. "I've got a carriage waiting outside."

"Fill me in."

Clint did, as they walked from the platform to the station, and then the station to the coach. Both men's eyes were alert the entire way. Finally, they were in the coach and heading for the Alhambra. It was an enclosed coach, so no one could see them from the outside.

Doc took a moment to cough into his handkerchief when they were seated.

"How are you doing, Doc?" Clint asked.

"Coughing up mah lungs, as usual," Doc said, with his slight Southern accent.

"I heard you spent some time in one of those sanitoriums."

"Got tired of sitting around all day waiting to die," Doc said. "I'd rather have it happen while I'm on the move, preferably from a bullet."

Clint stared at him.

"Don't worry," Doc said, "that doesn't mean I intend

to step in front of one. It's still gonna have to find me.''

"That's good to hear.''

"Although, from what you tell me,'' Doc said, "that may be even sooner than I'd like.''

"They're called what?'' Doc asked as they were approaching the Alhambra.

"Well, that's what we've decided to call them,'' Clint said. Then in defense he added, "We've got to call them something.''

Doc took the business card from his vest pocket and looked at it.

"I guess it could mean that,'' he said. Then he repeated, "Circle of Nine.''

"Where did you find it?''

"One of the men I killed had it on him, in his vest pocket.''

"How did it happen?''

"It was no big deal. I came out of a saloon in Virginia City and there were three of them waiting. They called me out loudly, made it sound as if it was a personal fight.''

"And?''

Doc's flat, expressionless eyes regarded Clint from beneath only slightly arched eyebrows.

"I killed them. If memory serves me, you also killed three.''

"Yes,'' Clint said, "and they sent three after Heck Thomas. He said he got lucky.''

"I didn't,'' Doc said, "and I doubt that you did, either. We just happen to be that good. What about Masterson?''

"Two.''

Doc frowned.

"Is it possible that somebody underestimated Bat Masterson?''

"Apparently so.''

"Then they're not beyond making mistakes," Doc Holliday said. "This is good."

Clint stared at the former dentist and wondered why he hadn't thought of that.

TWENTY-NINE

When they reached the Alhambra they checked Doc into the hotel.

"I'm embarrassed to say I'm not sure I can afford this place," Doc said as they crossed the lobby.

"That won't be a problem."

"Why not?"

"I can get them to give you a complimentary room."

"And how will you work that out?"

"Do you know Donald Frate?"

"Not the man, but I know the name. Is he running this operation?"

"He is, and he's going to be getting up a high-stakes game for Bat. We can just add you to the game."

"Did I come here to play poker?" Doc asked.

"No, and neither did Bat. Let's get you checked in and I'll explain."

Luckily, Harold was on desk duty, and he checked Doc in on Clint's say-so. Also, he was as impressed with Doc Holliday as he was with Clint and Bat.

In the lobby of the hotel Doc suddenly seemed to wilt. The trip had been long and his cough was becoming persistent.

"You should probably rest after your trip," Clint said. "I could take your bag up to your room for you—"

"I'm sure the hotel has someone who can do that," Holliday said, looking at Harold.

"Oh, yes, sir," he said. "I'll have a bellboy right here."

"Thank you," Doc said, and looked at Clint. "See? But you are right, I would like to rest for a little while."

"Well, you let me know when, and I'll have Heck and Bat here. We can have dinner in the dining room here and discuss our tactics."

"That sounds just fine," Doc said. "How about eight-thirty?"

"Eight-thirty's good."

A bellboy appeared and picked up Doc's bag.

"Right this way, sir."

"I'll see you at eight-thirty," Doc said to Clint. "Thanks for the ride from the station."

"No problem," Clint said. "I'm glad you're here, Doc. The four of us should be able to get to the bottom of this."

"Ah sincerely hope so."

Clint watched as Doc followed the bellboy up the stairs to the next level, then turned and looked at Harold.

"Is Mr. Frate around?"

"I believe he's in his office, sir."

"Would you tell him I'd like to see him? Tell him I'll buy him a drink in the saloon."

"Yes, sir, I'll tell him."

"Thanks, Harold."

Clint was reminded that he still had something to settle with Harold, but this was not the time. He nodded and headed for the saloon.

THIRTY

Clint was pleased to see Frate enter the saloon just fifteen minutes later. He was probably eager to set up the high-stakes game.

"Have a drink?" Clint asked as Frate joined him at the bar.

In reply Frate lifted a finger to the bartender, who brought over what appeared to be a snifter full of brandy. Clint wondered if Frate had been a brandy drinker before he took over the Alhambra operation.

"Have you talked to Bat about the game?"

"I have."

"Is he for it?"

"He's all for it . . . but he wanted me to tell you that he wants a truly high-stakes game. No pikers. No beginners. He wants men with money who know how to play the game."

"You'd think he'd want some beginners with money," Frate said.

"Bat likes to test his skills, Mr. Frate," Clint said. "He's not just in it for the money."

"Very well," Frate said. "Five-card stud?"

"What else?"

117

"I'll come up with eight more players."

"Seven."

"Why—"

"I have another player for you," Clint said. "He just arrived."

"And who is that?"

"John Holliday."

Frate's eyes widened.

"Doc Holliday?"

"Yes."

"But . . ."

"But what?"

Frate lowered his voice.

"He's crazy, isn't he?"

"Not at all," Clint said. "He's ill, but he's not crazy. Where'd you get that idea?"

"Well," Frate said, "everybody says—"

"Don't believe what everybody says, Frate," Clint said. "You'll get in trouble that way."

"You're probably right."

Clint thought he saw Frate's hand trembling as he drank his brandy—or was he mistaken?

"By the way, I told Harold you'd give Doc a free room while he played in the game."

"Of course."

"And you'll pick up Bat's room, too?"

"Yes," Frate said, "as for yours—"

"I'm not in the game," Clint said, "there's no need to pay for my room."

"That's all right," Frate said. "It's done."

"You can speak for the hotel?"

"I'll take care of it."

"Good," Clint said. "When can you put this all together by?"

"Tomorrow night," Frate said, as if it were a foregone conclusion.

"That's fine."

"Just sign for your meals and drinks while you're in the hotel from now on," Frate said, putting his snifter down on the bar. "It's all taken care of."

"Thank you, Mr. Frate," Clint said. "We all appreciate that."

"Around midday tomorrow I'll verify the game with, uh, you? Or Bat? Or—"

"With me is fine," Clint said. "I might as well act as their agent in this."

"Very well," Frate said. "I'll see you tomorrow."

"Have a nice evening, Mr. Frate."

"Uh, yes, you, too," Frate said, "and a lucky one."

Clint found Bat playing blackjack somewhat listlessly—so much so that he quit as soon as Clint appeared.

"I'm hungry."

"Wait until eight-thirty," Clint said. "Another forty minutes."

"Why eight-thirty?"

"That's when Doc will come down."

"He's here already?"

"Yes."

"How is he?"

"He's a little weak," Clint said. "He needed about an hour's rest."

"I hope he can last."

"He'll last," Clint said. "Come on, we'll wait in the dining room."

"What about Heck?"

"He'll find us."

They walked to the dining room and secured a table for four.

When they had a pot of coffee between them, Clint relayed to Bat his conversation with Doc.

"So he's in with us."

"Definitely."

"Good."

"I also spoke to Frate about the game."

"And?"

"He'll have seven more players by tomorrow night . . . he says."

"He will," Bat said. "He's probably got a long list of high rollers looking for a game with the likes of me or Doc."

"He was surprised Doc wanted to play."

"Why?"

"He's apparently under the impression that Doc's, uh, crazy."

"Doc?" Bat asked, feigning shock. "What ever gave him a crazy idea like that?"

"Beats me."

"I guess he believes what he reads."

"And hears."

"Did you ask Doc about Wyatt's whereabouts?"

"No," Clint said. "Didn't get a chance."

"Well, we can ask him when he gets here," Bat said. "For all we know this Circle of Nine killed him already."

"I think if Wyatt Earp was dead," Clint said, "we'd have heard about it by now."

"You're probably right. Here's Heck," Bat said, as Heck was approaching their table.

"Order yet?"

"We're waiting for Doc."

"He's here already?"

Clint nodded.

"How is he?"

"We just went through that," Bat said. "Apparently he's

fine, and ready to see this through with us.''

Clint told Heck about his conversation with Doc, and then with Frate. By the time Doc appeared they were all caught up.

As Doc approached the table all three men stood up. Doc shook hands with Bat, then turned and was introduced to Heck.

"I've heard a lot about you," Doc said. "I'm glad you're in on this.''

"Likewise.''

Both Bat and Heck watched carefully as Doc sat down. Doc's color was bad, almost yellow, and his eyes were watery.

"Don't worry, gentlemen," Doc said, without looking at them, "I'm not going to keel over. I need some whiskey and food, and I'll be fine.''

"Sure, Doc," Bat said, and beckoned to a waiter. When the man came over to take their order, he seemed nervous to be serving a table occupied by men with four of the biggest reputations in the West.

Clint noticed the waiter's nervousness and realized—by watching the man's darting eyes—that the man he feared most seemed to be Doc.

He must have thought Doc was crazy.

THIRTY-ONE

The four men sat and strategized in the dining room until well past ten-thirty. They went through several pots of coffee, a couple of slices of pie each—except for Doc, who went through several glasses of whiskey, which were making his already glazed eyes that much more glassy.

"Well, then," Doc said finally, "as I understand it my job is to watch Bat's back, and his is to watch mine."

"That's right," Clint said.

"If that sits right with you, Doc," Bat said.

"Only one," Doc said, then looked at Clint and added, "or two men I'd rather have watching my back, Bat."

"Speaking of which," Bat said, "we've been trying to locate Wyatt, Doc. Any ideas?"

"Wyatt still has some personal business to attend to as a result of Tombstone, Bat," Doc said.

"We heard you were part of that personal business, Doc," Clint said.

"Some of it," Doc said, but didn't elaborate. "If you gents don't mind, I'm going to get a good night's sleep under my belt if we're going to be playing high-stakes poker tomorrow."

"Sure, Doc," Clint said.

123

Doc stood up, then looked around the table.

"Nobody minds if I play to win, do they?" he asked.

"I'd prefer it, Doc," Bat said. "It'll make the game more interesting."

"Until tomorrow, then," Doc said, and left the table. He headed in a more or less straight line to the door with only the hint of a weave or two.

"He can hold his liquor, can't he?" Heck asked, shaking his head.

"I think it helps him with the coughing," Clint commented.

"Can't be doing his liver all that much good, though," Bat said.

"I don't think Doc's worried about his liver, Bat," Clint said. "I think he knows it's going to outlast him."

"Must be hell, just waiting around to die," Heck said.

"Hell," Bat replied, "that's what we're all doing, isn't it?"

"Yeah, but you, me, Clint here," Heck said, "it'll probably happen quick, from a bullet. I prefer that to the way he's going."

"He'd prefer that, too, Heck," Clint said. "If you boys don't mind, I think we should stick together for a while."

"Start watching each other's backs as of tonight, huh?" Bat asked.

"That's the idea."

"Well, who's for some gambling, huh?" Bat asked.

"Not me," Heck said. "I'm gonna head back to my hotel and do what Doc's doing."

"Why don't you do it right here?" Clint said. "We can squeeze another room out of them, or you can bunk on the sofa in my room."

"You got a sofa in your room?" Bat asked.

"A small one," Clint said.

"How'd you rate that?"

"I don't know," Clint said. "Lucky, I guess. Heck?"

"I'm too tired to argue, and too tired to walk back to my hotel," Heck said. "I'll take your sofa and then you can get me a room tomorrow. I might as well take advantage of all these free services you boys are getting."

They all stood up.

"And what are you boys gonna do with the rest of the evening?" Heck asked.

"Gamble," Bat said.

"A bit," Clint said. "I might have something better to do."

They went out to the lobby and Clint got Heck an extra key to his room from the desk clerk, whom he didn't recognize. Heck took the key, bade them good night, and went up.

"Something better to do?" Bat asked. "With Heck in your room?"

"I didn't think of that," Clint said. "Say—"

"Oh, no you don't," Bat said. "I'm not giving you my room. You and your lady friend will have to make other arrangements."

"Speaking of my lady friend," Clint said, "she still wants to meet you."

"Sure," Bat said, "I'll let you introduce us. That'll just impress her more, for you."

"I think she's impressed enough, thanks."

"I don't want to hear it," Bat said. "I think I feel like some faro tonight."

"Here, or somewhere else?"

"Here," Bat said. "We probably shouldn't make a habit of walking these streets at night."

"I don't know why," Clint said as they walked toward the casino. "Bushwhacking doesn't seem to be this Circle of Nine's style."

"Still," Bat said, "I don't want to be available when they decide to start."

"You've got a good point there, Bat," Clint admitted. "A good point."

THIRTY-TWO

Aaron Semple finished writing the last line of his journal entry and then closed the book and put it in the bottom drawer of his desk. On the cover of the book was a circle with the number nine in it.

The "Circle of Nine" had been Semple's idea, one that he had quickly been able to sell to eight colleagues of his. He proposed to them that the Old West was quickly dying, and that there was money to be made in that. Investment opportunities connected to the death of the Old West and the coming turning of the century—albeit still a good fifteen or sixteen years away. Still, it was time to plan for that glorious time—and since Semple was only forty-five, he was sure that he would still be going strong when 1900 rolled around.

"Darling?"

He looked up from his desk and saw his wife standing in the doorway. At forty-two she had, for some reason, lost the looks that had attracted him when she was thirty. After twelve years of marriage, he had grown tired of her. Still, she *was* a good hostess, and many of their friends were just that, "their" friends, so divorce was out of the question, just now.

"Yes, dear?"

"Are you going out tonight?"

"Yes, dear."

"Gambling?"

"Mmm-hmmm."

He stood up and she could see that he was wearing his best tuxedo—just to go gambling?

"Will you be out late?"

"Possibly," he said, approaching her. He paused to give her a quick peck on the cheek and then continued to the front door and out.

Virginia Semple was still a vibrant woman at forty-two, still beautiful to everyone but her husband. Her body was firm, her face still attractive, but she *was* forty-two, something that Aaron seemed unable to forgive her for. He preferred younger women—not *much* younger women, but younger all the same.

It used to bother Virginia, but months ago she had decided that two could play at that game. Now that her husband was gone for the evening—and most of the night, no doubt—she went upstairs to prepare herself for her twenty-four-year-old lover, who would be arriving shortly.

When they entered the casino Clint saw Deborah right away, despite the fact that she was wearing a blue dress tonight, not a red one. She was not, however, surrounded by a group of men, but was rather draped on the arm of a single man.

Apparently, tonight she was working.

"What is it?" Bat asked.

"The lady who wants to meet you."

"Where?"

"Over there, at the roulette table, with the blue dress."

"The one showing a lot of, uh, chest?"

"That's her."

"She's with someone."

"Yes," Clint said, "tonight. I guess she'll have to wait to meet you."

"Why? I'm sure her escort wouldn't mind." Bat said. "Besides, he looks like he has a lot of money."

"You mean . . ."

"Who knows?"

"Okay, then," Clint said, "let's go and make the introduction."

They descended the steps to the casino floor and headed for the roulette wheel.

When Deborah saw Clint approaching, her stomach lurched. She had tried to get out of this engagement tonight, but this particular man was difficult to say no to. For the first time in her life, though, she felt ashamed of her chosen profession.

"What is it, dear?" the man asked.

"Nothing."

The man saw the other two men approaching.

"Do you know these men?"

"One of them. He's a . . . friend."

A smile creased the man's face.

"A jealous lover, perhaps?"

"I don't think so."

"A pity," he said. "A little excitement would have livened up the night."

He turned his attention back to the roulette wheel, where he was betting obscene amounts of money on single numbers, after getting the okay to do so from Donald Frate. He and Frate were, after all, not only friends, they belonged to the same club.

Deborah watched as Clint came closer and suddenly realized who the other more dapperly dressed man was.

Apparently, she was about to meet the infamous Bat Masterson.

THIRTY-THREE

"Deborah," Clint said, "how nice to run into you."

"Clint, hello," she said.

The man she was with was watching the roulette wheel turn. Clint had the impression that he and Bat were being deliberately ignored.

"I have someone I want you to meet," Clint said, "if this is convenient?"

"Is this who I think it is?" she asked.

"Deborah Whitcomb," Clint said, making it official, "this is Bat Masterson."

"A pleasure," Bat said, reaching for her hand, but abruptly her escort turned to face them, staring directly at Bat.

"Did you say Bat Masterson?" he asked.

"That's right," Bat replied.

"Deborah," the man said, "you didn't tell me you knew Bat Masterson."

"I don't," she said, "I mean, I didn't, until right now. I know this other gentleman, Clint Adams."

Now her escort turned his eyes on Clint.

"The Gunsmith?"

Clint wished the man hadn't said it so loud. People were looking now.

"This is amazing," the man said, "to see you both in the same place."

"I was making an introduction to the lady," Clint said quietly.

"Oh, of course," the man said, "pardon my rudeness. Please, complete your introduction."

Bat took Deborah's hand and kissed it, then said, "Clint's description did not do you justice. You're very beautiful."

"Thank you, Mr. Masterson," she said. "It's a great pleasure to meet you."

"And now, my dear," the man said, "would you introduce me to your two friends?"

"Mr. Masterson—"

"Bat, please."

"Bat, Clint," Deborah said, "I'd like to present Mr. Aaron Semple."

"I don't know the name," Bat said. "Should I?"

"Only if you were from San Francisco," Semple said, "and involved with banking."

"Well," Bat said, "I'm involved with money, but not banking."

"Well," Semple said, "actually, we both do the same thing with money."

"We do?"

"Of course," Semple said, "we gamble with it."

"The difference is," Bat said, "I gamble with my own money."

"Touché, Mr. Masterson," Semple said. "Or shall I call you Bat?"

"You can call me Mr. Masterson," Bat said, because he had disliked the man on the spot. Clint could see that the feeling was mutual. In fact, he didn't like Aaron Semple much, either.

"Well," Clint said, "we'll leave you to your roulette

wheel. I know how much you like playing."

"Oh, I'm not playing tonight," she said, "I'm just watching."

"She's my good luck," Semple said, patting the hand that was on his arm. Clint noticed that the man was wearing a wedding ring.

"Your wife doesn't bring you luck?" Bat asked, because he had noticed the ring, also.

"None at all," the man said, without the slightest hint of discomfort at the question. "In fact, my wife hates gambling, so she brings me nothing but bad luck."

"Too bad," Bat said.

"Going to do some gambling yourself while you're here, Mr. Masterson?" Semple asked.

"Some."

"Any particular game?"

"Poker is my game, sir," Bat said, "although I was thinking about faro, tonight. If you'll excuse me, I'll see if I can find a place. Miss Whitcomb, a pleasure."

"Please," she said, "call me Deborah."

"I will," Bat said. "I promise." He turned to Clint. "See you later."

Bat moved into the crowd around them, and people who thought there might be some sort of confrontation turned away disappointed and returned to their own gambling.

"Well," Semple said, "he doesn't seem a very friendly sort."

"He is, to his friends," Clint said.

"No chance of that happening, I'm afraid. I suppose it's my manner. I've been told I am, on occasion, rude."

"Who told you a thing like that?" Clint asked.

"My wife, I'm afraid," Semple said. "No one else would have the nerve."

"Ah, is that because you're an important man?" Clint

asked. "Or were you speaking of people who work for you?"

"Some people consider me important," Semple said, "and I do have a lot of people working for me."

"I see. Well, if you'll both excuse me, I think I'll try to find a game."

"And what is your game, Mr. Gunsmith?"

"My game, Mr. Banker," Clint said, "is seeing how long I can go without having someone call me that. Good evening."

THIRTY-FOUR

Aaron Semple was perturbed.

He had been shocked to find Bat Masterson and Clint Adams in the same casino as he was. They were both supposed to be dead. Granted, the initial attempts on their lives had failed, but they were supposed to have been taken care of by now. Someone had made a bad mistake, and they were going to be sorry.

He had to leave and call an emergency meeting of the Circle of Nine.

Clint was watching Bat play faro when he felt a tap on his shoulder. He turned and was pleasantly surprised to find Deborah Whitcomb standing there.

"Where's your escort?" he asked, looking over her lovely, bare shoulders.

"He suddenly decided he had to leave."

"When did that happen?"

"Right after he met you two. I think you scared him away."

Bat heard her and turned away from the table.

"Mr. Semple didn't strike me as the type to scare," he said. "Maybe he was just . . . surprised."

135

Clint looked at Bat and knew what he was suggesting. Semple was a banker. Did that mean he was wealthy?

"Tell me, Deborah," Clint said, "does Mr. Semple have money?"

"Loads of it," she said. "He was born into a fortune, and then proceeded to double it and triple it."

"What's his reputation in San Francisco?" Bat asked.

"They tell me that he's ruthless when it comes to making money."

Clint and Bat exchanged a glance. Was there money to be made in having them, and men like them, killed?

"What is it?" she asked.

"Nothing," Clint said.

"We just didn't like him," Bat said.

"Well, to tell you the truth," she said, "I don't like him much myself."

"Then why were you with him?" Bat asked.

"Didn't you hear me?" she asked. "I said he had loads of money."

"Oh, right," Bat said. "Sorry."

"Anyway," she said to Clint, "I'm not busy now. I thought maybe . . . we could have a drink?"

"I don't think—"

"Go on, my children," Bat said, interrupting. "Have a drink."

"Bat—"

"I'll be right here," Bat said. "You can see me from the bar."

"All right," Clint said, and smiled at Deborah. "A drink."

They walked to the small bar area, got a table from which Clint could see the entire floor—and Bat—and ordered drinks—wine for her, beer for him.

"I didn't really mean drinks," Deborah said in a conspiratorial whisper.

"I know what you meant," Clint said. "I'm just—uh, I have a guest in my room tonight."

"Oh?" Deborah asked. "Another woman, already?"

"Why not?" he asked. "You were on the arm of another man."

"That was business."

"So is this," Clint said. "My guest is Heck Thomas."

"The detective?"

"That's right."

"Aren't you friends?"

"We are," Clint said, "so it's actually business and pleasure."

"The kind of business where you have to be able to see Bat at all times, and he has to be able to see you?" she asked.

"Yes," Clint said, "that kind of business."

"How exciting. What is it about?"

Clint continued to look at Bat's back as he considered how to answer her question.

"Does it have something to do with Aaron?"

"Possibly," Clint said, "although I didn't think that before tonight—but then, I didn't know him before tonight."

"So now you suspect him of something because you didn't like him?"

"No," Clint said, "because he has loads of money."

"So you don't like him because he's rich?"

"I don't mind rich people," Clint said. "It's the ones who think they can get away with anything that get me upset."

"I see," she said. "And what's Aaron supposed to be getting away with?"

"I don't know," Clint said. "I might know more tomorrow, though."

"So I gather that you and I won't be . . ."

"Not tonight, I'm afraid."

''Well,'' she said, ''dumped twice in one night.''

''That's not fair—''

She laughed.

''Take it easy,'' she said. ''I'm just teasing. I'm perfectly happy to sit here with you and talk awhile, and then I think I'll retire to bed and let you and your friend Bat have your adventure.''

Thinking of her in her bed made Clint think of another kind of adventure he'd rather be having, and he said so.

''You're a sweet man, Clint,'' she said, and told him her room number.

Just in case.

THIRTY-FIVE

Clint apologized to Deborah for not being able to escort her to her room.

"You boys may not be safe in this hotel," she said, "but I am. Besides, if you did escort me to my room you wouldn't be back down here—I guarantee it."

Clint believed it, and wished for it. He took his eyes off of Bat long enough to watch her walk to the door, as did every other man in the place.

When she was gone he ordered another beer. He decided to simply stay where he was. His mind was not on gambling and, he could see, neither was Bat's. Essentially, they were putting themselves out there as bait, but no one seemed to be biting. Finally, toward the end of the evening—actually, it was morning—Bat left the faro table and came over to the bar to join Clint.

"Nobody's going to try anything in here," Bat said.

"I don't see why not," Clint said. "Every other try has been reasonably public."

"Except for the try on Heck."

"That's true," Clint said, "but he was out walking track."

"Yes," Bat said, "but they seem to want witnesses to

what they're doing. Why didn't they try for him while the railroad man was there?''

Clint and Bat suddenly looked into each other's eyes.

"Railroad men have money," Bat said.

"Do you think . . . ?"

"Maybe."

"In the morning we'll have to get his name from Heck," Clint said, "then we can check him out."

"But now?"

"We'll start with Rick Hartman," Clint said, "and then we'll see if the railroad man has any connection with Aaron Semple."

"A railroad man and a banker," Bat said. "You'd think they'd go hand in hand, wouldn't you?"

"Yes," Clint said, "I would."

"Or maybe we're reaching."

"Why not reach?" Clint asked. "We don't have anything else to go on yet."

Bat looked at his watch.

"I'd better turn in," Bat said. "I've got a big game starting tomorrow."

"All right," Clint said.

They got up and left together. Walking through the lobby Bat said, "I wonder if Heck snores."

"I'll let you know."

"Or you could spend the night somewhere else," Bat said. "If you're right about them wanting witnesses, then we're safe in our rooms. Once I'm in mine you could go to any room you like."

"You have a point there," Clint said.

So Bat went to his room, and Clint went elsewhere.

Although technically it was morning, it was early morning. Clint had a feeling that he wouldn't be disturbing Deborah if he knocked on her door. He turned out to be right. She answered the door wearing a filmy dressing gown which, while it covered her, managed to show off her luxurious flesh.

"Oh," he said, "are you not alone?"

She smiled, reached for him, drew him into the room and said, "I'm not now."

Her filmy nightgown came apart in his hands, and then she popped a couple of buttons on his shirt, and they were both naked. He pushed her onto the bed on her belly, then stopped her from turning over. He turned his attention to her plump buttocks, running his hands over them, his mouth, his tongue, licking the cleft between them, then parting her cheeks and probing with his tongue until she was gasping for air. He turned her over then and kissed her belly, and her thighs, then buried his face in her crotch and ate avidly until she cried out and tried to push his head away because the pleasure he was giving her was too intense.

He raised himself above her then and in spite of her protests—she said she was too sensitive "down there" for anything else—he held her arms down, pressed the tip of his penis to her moist vagina, and then plunged it home. She gasped, arching her back, but when he released her arms instead of trying to push him off she clasped him to her so that he couldn't have gotten off of her if he wanted to.

Which he didn't.

He rode her hard, all the way to her completion, then continued on until his own pleasure came rushing out in an explosion that made him bellow like a wounded bull, and then collapsed on her.

"I'm heavy," he said moments later. But she wrapped her arms around him and said, "No."

They actually fell asleep like that.

•   •   •

Sometime during the night he had rolled off of her and lay beside her. He awoke before dawn and looked down at her lying on her belly.

At different times in his life he had found various parts of a woman's body more beautiful than others. Once it was their navels; another time their bellies; there was a time when he actually found women's armpits extremely sexy; shoulders; breasts; feet once. This morning he thought that he had never seen anything as beautiful in his life as Deborah Whitcomb's ass.

He reclined there on one elbow, staring at it until the sun came up.

THIRTY-SIX

"Parsons," Heck Thomas said at breakfast, "his name is Wesley Parsons, president of the Pacific Coast Railroad. Why?"

Clint and Bat exchanged a glance, and it was Clint who explained their theory.

"You think you can connect a banker you don't like to a railroad man and then connect them to this Circle of Nine?" Heck asked then.

"They're money men, Heck," Bat reminded him. "Both of them."

"I know that, but . . . it just sounds like a stretch to me."

"You're the detective," Clint said, "we're not. How many times have you stretched for a truth and found it?"

"A lot," Heck admitted.

"That's all we're doing," Clint said, "trying to stretch for a truth."

"What do you think, Doc?" Bat asked.

Today Doc's color was much better, and he was actually eating the same steak and eggs breakfast the others were.

"I think maybe we're thinking about this a little too much."

"Meaning?" Bat asked.

"Meaning if they want us, they'll come after us," Doc said, "eventually."

"While we're all together?" Heck asked.

"If it's the only way," Doc said, "Yes. They might even take it as a challenge."

"I think Doc has a point," Bat said.

"So do I," Clint said, "but that doesn't mean I want to just sit back and wait."

"Well," Bat said, "as of tonight Doc and I will be in a high-stakes poker game with a room full of money men. Maybe this fella we met last night, Semple, will even be one of them."

"They're not gonna try anything," Doc said. "They're not gunmen. The ones who will be in danger then will be Clint and Heck. They'll be on the outside."

"Doc's right again," Heck said, looking across the table at Clint. "You and I are gonna have to stick together like glue."

"I don't have a problem with that, Heck," Clint said. "But I'll still want to move around."

"Doing what?"

"First I want to check on Wesley Parsons, then Aaron Semple."

"How do we do that?" Heck asked.

"Do you know a detective in San Francisco?" Clint asked. "I used to know a couple, but they're not here anymore."

"I might know a couple," Heck said, "but we might have the same problem. I don't know if they're still here."

"If they're not," Clint said, "I'll send a telegram to Talbot Roper. He can recommend somebody."

"I thought you didn't want to get him involved?" Bat asked.

"I don't," Clint said. "I'm just going to ask him to give us a name."

"You know Roper," Bat said. "He'll want to come out here."

"I can keep him away," Clint said.

Bat shrugged.

"You do know him better than I do."

"Didn't you say something about a kid who works here knowing something?" Heck asked him.

"Yes, the head desk clerk, Harold," Clint said. "He about swallowed his tongue when I showed him the Circle-Nine card."

"Then I guess we'd better start by asking him some questions."

"Right," Clint said, "only I think Doc should do it."

"Why Doc?" Bat asked.

"Have you noticed the trouble the waiter has in serving him? Doc is scarier than we are."

Doc smiled then and said, "That's because everybody thinks I'm crazy."

"Right," Clint said, "and we might as well use that to our best advantage."

THIRTY-SEVEN

They decided after breakfast that Clint and Doc should go talk to Harold, which meant that Heck and Bat would cover each other's back for a while.

When they got to the lobby they split up, and Clint and Doc went to the front desk, where they found Harold working.

"Hello, Harold," Clint said.

"Good morning, Mr. Adams."

"You remember Doc Holliday," Clint said.

"I sure do!" Harold said, and his eyes widened as he looked at Doc. Doc was slight and blond and knew that when people met him they expected him to be bigger. When they got over his lack of size, though, they still feared his reputation.

"I hope you're enjoying your stay at the Alhambra, sir."

"Harold," Clint said, "it's time for us to finish our talk."

"Our . . . talk?"

"You'd better get someone to handle the desk for you," Clint suggested.

"Oh, but I can't," Harold said, "I have to, uh, I'm very busy—"

"Just do what the man says, Harold," Doc said menacingly. "Don't make me pull you out from behind that desk."

Harold looked at Doc, and Clint thought he could hear the younger man swallow.

"I, uh, will just be a minute."

"There's a good lad," Doc said.

They waited while Harold fetched a young man to spell him, and then he came around the desk.

"Where should we go, Harold?" Clint asked. "You don't want anyone to see us talking in earnest, do you?"

"Um, the same café as yesterday?"

"Why not? You lead the way."

When they reached the café they got a table and the three of them had coffee. Clint and Doc weren't hungry because they had had breakfast, and Harold was feeling too sick to eat.

"Harold," Clint said, putting the Circle-Nine card on the table as he had done yesterday, "the last time I showed you this card you got agitated. You got up and almost ran out of here."

"No, I, uh, didn't, uh, I had to go—"

"Just relax, kid," Doc Holliday said. "Nobody's gonna hurt you . . . unless you don't tell us what we want to know."

Harold looked imploringly at Clint.

"I could get in trouble," he said.

"You could get worse," Doc said.

"Mr. Adams—"

"Just tell us where you've seen this card before, Harold."

Harold stared at the card as sweat formed on his brow and started to roll down his temples.

"Come on . . ." Doc growled.

"I have seen that card before," Harold finally said, "but I don't know what it means."

"That's all right," Clint said. "We'll figure out what it means. Just tell us where you've seen it before."

"I saw it somewhere . . . I wasn't supposed to be," Harold said. "If he finds out he'll fire me."

"Damn it, Harold!" Doc snapped, making the young man jump.

"In Mr. Frate's office!" he said hurriedly.

"What?" Clint asked.

"I saw it in Mr. Frate's office."

"Where in his office?"

"On his desk."

"Do you know if it was his?"

"No," Harold said, "I only saw it on his desk. I wasn't supposed to be in his office. I just . . . wanted to sit behind his big desk when he wasn't there. Please, don't tell him!"

"I'm not going to tell him, Harold," Clint said, "but where else have you seen it?"

"Where else?"

"Yes," Clint said. "I get the feeling you're only telling me half the truth, Harold. Am I right about that, hmm?"

"Oh, gee—"

"Is that right, Harold?" Doc asked.

Harold closed his eyes.

"Mr. Semple."

"Aaron Semple?" Clint asked. "The banker?"

Harold nodded again.

"What about him?" Clint asked.

"He carries one."

"You've seen it on him?"

Harold nodded again.

"When? How?"

"One morning he was paying a bill at the desk. He'd

taken a room for the night, you see, to be with . . . a woman who wasn't his wife.''

"We don't care about that, Harold," Doc said. "We don't care who the man sleeps with."

"Well," Harold said, "he was taking some cash out of his wallet and something fell out. I started to pick it up for him to, you know, be helpful, and he shouted at me not to touch it.''

"But you saw it," Clint said.

Harold nodded.

"And it was this card?''

"Yes," Harold said, "it was just like that one. He picked it up from the floor and put it back in his wallet quickly. Then he gave me a big tip.''

"To keep your mouth shut.''

"I guess.''

"And you never told anyone?''

"Even if he hadn't tipped me," Harold said, "who would I have told, and why? The card meant nothing to me.''

"Where did you see it first, Harold?" Clint asked.

"First on Mr. Frate's desk, and then when Mr. Semple dropped it.''

Clint and Doc exchanged a look.

"Frate could have got it from Semple for some reason," Doc said.

"Maybe," Clint said. "At least we know Semple had it on his person. This explains why he acted so surprised to see me and Bat last night.''

"You were supposed to be dead.''

"Dead?" Harold asked.

"Harold, I'm going to do what Mr. Semple did," Clint said.

"What's . . . that?''

"I'm going to give you a big tip to forget this ever happened. Can you do that?"

"S-sure."

Clint took some money from his pocket and gave it to the younger man.

"T-thanks, Mr. Adams."

Harold stood up.

"Harold," Doc said.

"Yes, sir?"

"If you don't forget about this . . ."

"Oh, I will, I will," Harold said quickly. "I promise, sir."

Doc stared at him, then nodded.

"All right," Clint said.

"May I go now? I have to get back to work."

"Yes, Harold," Doc said. "Go."

Once again Harold almost ran from the café.

"This connects Frate and Semple," Doc said, "even more than as the manager of the casino and a customer."

"I wonder in what other way they're connected," Clint said.

"That's what we're gonna find out," Doc said, "isn't it?"

THIRTY-EIGHT

In the end Clint did have to send a telegram to Talbot Roper to get the name of a San Francisco private detective. The two Heck knew of were no longer in business; one had left town, the other was dead.

The name Roper gave them was Dominick Polo, whose father had come to America from Italy, worked on the railroads, and then became a policeman. Polo was also a policeman in San Francisco for a short time, but then quit and opened his own office. Talbot said in the telegram that the man was good and could be trusted.

Clint and Doc sat before his small desk in his small office on Market Street.

"I don't spend a lot of money on office space," Polo said. "I'm rarely here. Wouldn't be here with you today if I hadn't gotten a telegram from Tal Roper. Understand you're a good friend of his, Mr. Adams."

"That's right."

"Well, I've learned a lot from Roper," Polo said. "I owe him, so what can I do for you?"

"We need you to check on a man for us."

"Who?" Polo picked up a pencil to write the name down.

"Aaron Semple."

Polo put down the pencil and sat back in his chair. He was in his thirties, with dark black hair and an air of competence about him.

"You know the name," Clint said.

"Of course," Polo said. "Everyone knows his name. He's a wealthy man."

"Does that mean you won't do it?" Doc asked.

"Oh, no, I'll do it," Polo said. "Because I owe Talbot Roper I'll do it, even though Semple could put me out of business with a snap of his fingers if he found out I was running a check on him."

"Look," Clint said, "I don't want you to risk your business. Come on, Doc—"

"Wait a minute, Clint," Doc said, putting his hand on Clint's arm and then leaning forward. "It's people's lives we're talking about, Polo. Not only ours, but many others."

Polo folded his hands in his lap and regarded Doc quizzically for a moment.

"Suppose you tell me exactly what's going on," he said then.

Clint explained the situation to Polo while Doc sat by silently. Clint appreciated the fact that the detective was unimpressed with Doc and him, or, if he was impressed, he wasn't showing it.

When Clint finished he gave Polo a chance to digest it all.

"I'll see what I can dig up on Semple, and a possible connection to both Parsons and Frate. I can get in touch with you at the Alhambra?"

"Yes, but don't leave any messages," Clint said. "They might find their way back to Frate."

Polo nodded.

"I'll be in touch."

"You can talk to me, Doc, Bat Masterson, or Heck Thomas."

Polo nodded.

"I'd like to meet Thomas," he said, finally looking impressed with someone.

"That can be easily arranged," Clint said.

"Good, Give me a day or two."

Clint stood up, followed by Doc.

"If we have that long."

The three men shook hands and then Clint and Doc left.

"What did you think?" Clint asked when they were outside.

Doc hesitated just a moment and then said, "He'll do."

THIRTY-NINE

The poker game began at eight p.m. It was held in a private room in the hotel, a room Clint and Heck weren't allowed inside because they weren't playing.

It was seven-thirty and the four men were in the dining room.

"Have you talked with Frate?" Clint asked Bat. "Found out who the other players are?"

"No," Bat said.

"Doc?"

"I've been with you."

"There was a message at the desk for me with the room number," Bat said.

"What if it's a trap?" Heck asked. "I mean, if we suspect Frate of anything we should be careful where two of us go."

"I agree," Clint said. "I think we should all walk up to this room. If it's a trap, let's all fall into it."

Doc smiled.

"What?"

"Don't think there's a trap in the world could close on the four of us," he said. "Not in a hotel."

Clint thought that this was the kind of bravado that got

157

men killed, but he didn't say anything. In this particular instance, he agreed with Doc's assessment. Forty men out in the street would kill the four of them easily, but he didn't think they could be taken in a hotel room. Heck was right about Frate. If they suspected him of any complicity, then they couldn't allow Bat and Doc to walk into that room without Clint and Heck to watch their backs.

"You won't be allowed to stay once the game begins," Bat said.

"That's okay," Clint said. "At least we can get a look at the room and the players before they kick us out."

"What makes you think Frate will even let us in?" Heck asked.

"Because he's been very cooperative up to this point," Clint said. "And he knows that men with reputations are careful men. He'll let us in, but we'll have to leave almost immediately."

"Tell him I'm crazy," Doc said.

"What?" Clint asked.

"He'll believe that," Doc said. "Tell him I want you to check under the table for guns."

"That's good," Bat said. "Tell him Doc and I don't want any guns in the room."

"Except yours?"

"That's right."

Clint smiled.

"That might work," he said. "That just might work."

Fifteen minutes later Clint was in Frate's office for an "emergency" meeting.

"He wants what?" Frate asked.

"He wants me to check the room to make sure it's safe," Clint said.

"Doc Holliday?"

"Well," Clint said, "it was Doc's idea, but Bat's going along with it."

"The men in this game are gentlemen," Frate said. "Bankers, politicians, brokers—"

"No reason they should have guns, then, is there?"

Frate frowned and said, "Well, no, I guess not."

"Fine," Clint said. "No guns."

"What about Holliday and Masterson?"

"Oh, they'll have their guns," Clint said. "You can't expect men of their reputation to go anywhere without their guns, can you?"

"But . . . in a room of gentlemen, with no guns?"

"I'll tell you what," Clint said. "I'll let you talk to Doc about it and then—"

"No, no," Frate said. "These men want this game. I can get them to go along."

"And I go in to check the room."

"All right . . . but you can't stay once the game begins."

"Agreed."

"Also, I will have two men outside the door at all times," Frate said, "for security reasons. They will be armed."

"Agreed."

Frate wasn't pleased with these eleventh hour shenanigans, but there was little he could do about it at this point.

"I have one thing to ask."

"What's that?" Clint asked.

"I need your assurance that Holliday won't, uh, I mean—"

"Kill anyone?"

"Well . . . yes."

"Don't worry," Clint said, "Bat will be there. He can control Doc."

"I mean . . . he won't go crazy if he loses?" Frate asked.

"Not at all," Clint said. "While Doc is not used to losing, it has happened."

"There will be a lot of important men in that room," Frate said.

"Look," Clint said, "you've made assurances to me, I'm making some to you. Doc Holliday is not going to kill anyone who doesn't try to kill him first. Deal?"

With a dubious look on his face Frate replied, "Deal."

FORTY

They met in the lobby: Clint, Bat, Doc, Heck, and Donald Frate with his two security men, each holding a rifle. Frate shook hands with all of them, but Clint noticed the tentative look in his eyes when faced with Doc Holliday. Even the security men seemed uneasy in Doc's presence. He wondered how many of the other men in the game would feel the same apprehension.

They all walked up to the room together, Frate explaining that the other players were already there, as well as the house dealer.

"This is it," Frate said, as they stopped in front of a door on the second floor. "What do you want to do?"

"I will go in with you and take a look around," Clint said. "Doc and Bat will wait in the hall with Heck."

"All right," Frate said. "Do you need to be introduced to all the players?"

"Me to them," Clint said, "but not the other way around. For now, I don't need to know their names. I just want to check the room."

"Are you, uh, going to check them for weapons?"

"Did you do that?"

"Yes."

161

"Are you satisfied that none of them have weapons?"
Clint asked.

"I am."

Since they didn't necessarily trust Frate, this didn't mean
much. However, Clint felt that he could better check a man
for weapons with his eyes than someone like Frate could
with his hands.

"I won't check them," he said.

Frate let out a relieved breath. He seemed to be genuinely
worried about offending these wealthy, important players.

"It would have been . . . embarrassing," the man said.

"But they would have put up with it in order to play in
the same game with Bat Masterson and Doc Holliday."

"Yes," Frate said, "I'm sure they would have."

"Well," Clint said, "there won't be any need to embar-
rass anyone. Shall we go in?"

Frate used his key to open the door, and they entered
together. It was a spacious two-room suite, and in the center
of one room a large, round table had been set up. Around
the table sat seven well-dressed, prosperous-looking men
and one man—the house dealer—less prosperous-looking.
Clint wasn't surprised to see that one of the players was
the banker, Aaron Semple.

"Gentlemen," Frate said as they entered, "this is Clint
Adams."

"Ah," Aaron Semple said, "I didn't know the infamous
Gunsmith would be playing in this game. Excellent."

"Sorry to disappoint you, Mr. Semple," Clint said, "but
I'm just here to check the room."

"Are Mr. Masterson and Mr. Holliday out in the hall?"
another man asked.

"They are, but they'll come in after I've checked the
room."

"Better to be safe than sorry, eh?" Semple asked.

"Exactly. Do any of you gentlemen have a gun on you?" he asked.

The men around the table looked at each other, then at him.

"Will you search us?" one of them asked.

"No, sir," Clint said, "I'll take your word for it."

Some of the men said they didn't have guns, and others simply shook their heads.

Clint took a turn around the room, looked out the window to see if there was a balcony or a low roof—there wasn't—then simply took a walk around the table of players. At one point he even bent over to glance under the table.

Some of the men fidgeted nervously, and Clint thought he'd be able to tell if any of them had lied about having a gun. Even if one of them did, however, and got away with it, one of these bank types with a gun would not be a threat to Bat *and* Doc.

"Satisfied?" Frate asked.

"Yes, thank you."

"Gentlemen," Frate said, "the game will begin momentarily. Here are the last two of our players."

Clint passed Doc and Bat on his way out, and as the door closed behind him he heard the beginning of the introductions.

Outside Heck said, "So?"

Clint beckoned Heck away from the two security men, who were positioned one on each side of the door.

"The room's clean, and I believe the men are, too."

"Did you know any of them?"

"Yes," Clint said. "Aaron Semple is in there."

"The banker you and Bat don't like?"

"Yes."

"You may have been right about him, then."

"Maybe."

"What about the others?"

"They all look like him," Clint said. "Prosperous and dressed very well—but apprehensive."

"It's that rep of Doc's," Heck said. "I bet that works really well for him in poker games."

"I suppose it does. Come on, we might as well go downstairs."

"To do what?"

"I don't know," Clint said. "We'll think of something."

FORTY-ONE

Clint and Heck remained in the hotel. They went into the casino to have a drink where there were plenty of people around.

"I'm starting to feel itchy," Heck said as they sat down.

"I know," Clint said. "Like somebody's watching."

"Like something's gonna happen."

"Soon."

"Yeah."

"I'll get us two beers."

Clint got up, walked to the bar, and returned with two full mugs of cold beer.

"The only question is," Heck continued, "what's gonna happen, and where?"

Clint sipped his beer and put it down.

"There're too many people in here for anything to happen," Clint said. "They want witnesses, but they don't want innocent bystanders killed."

"That means they're concerned about public opinion," Heck said. "Having someone innocent accidently killed by flying lead would affect that."

"So they're not going to touch us while we're here," Clint said.

"Unless they call us outside, like they did with Gordon."

"He was foolish to go out," Clint said. "He couldn't know what was out there waiting for him."

"Clint," Heck said, "if we're dangling ourselves as bait, we're going about it all wrong."

"I know," Clint said. "They're not going to try for two of us together."

"Doc and Bat are pretty safe in that room, don't you think?"

"Unless they've hidden weapons all over the room, yes, I do think so. Bat's going to do some talking during the game, see if he can't smoke somebody out."

"You and I are gonna have to split up," Heck said. "It's the only way to bring them out."

"Let's think about that for a minute."

"While we're thinking," Heck said, "there's something I don't understand."

"What's that?"

"Why they came after me," Heck said. "I don't have the rep you and Doc and Bat do, and some of the others."

"Somebody thinks you do."

"But my rep is not with a gun."

Clint frowned.

"You've got a point."

"So why me?"

"I don't know," Clint said. "You're the detective. Why you?"

"Maybe somebody's got a personal grudge against me."

"Because you put somebody away?"

"Could be."

"Then why all this?" Clint asked. "Why all the other killings? Why go after me and Doc and Bat?"

Heck sat forward, warming to his subject.

"Because you're high profile," Heck said. "Because by

going after the likes of you they put the attempts in the spotlight.''

"So when you're killed," Clint said, picking up the thread, "it just looks like another attempt.''

"And nobody suspects that it was personal.''

Clint sat back, frowning some more.

"Can it be that simple—and yet, not? I mean, would somebody go through all of this, hiring as many guns as they would have to hire to pull this off?''

"I guess," Heck Thomas said, "that would depend on how much money they had . . . and just how badly they wanted me dead.''

FORTY-TWO

Aaron Semple looked across the table at Bat Masterson, then to his right at Doc Holliday. Both men seemed deeply involved in the game and after just an hour of play were well ahead, but what kind of fool did they take him for? Somehow, they had figured out that the Circle of Nine was operating from San Francisco and they—along with Heck Thomas and Clint Adams—had come here to find out who was behind it. Wouldn't they be shocked to find out the reason for all this? Wouldn't his other Circle colleagues be interested, as well? No one knew Semple's personal agenda except for Semple himself. This was the way he always operated.

No one at this table knew everything that was going on, except him.

And the two most surprised men in town would probably be Clint Adams and Heck Thomas!

"Your bet, Mr. Semple," the dealer said.

Semple smiled and said, "Five hundred."

Clint and Heck were still having a drink when Clint saw Dominick Polo working his way through the crowd. He stood up and waved, and Polo came over. Clint introduced Polo to Heck.

"A beer?" Clint asked.

"Sure."

Polo sat with Heck while Clint went and got him a mug of beer.

"Out gambling tonight?" Heck asked.

"No," Polo said, "actually I was looking for you—well, one of you."

"Well, you found two of us," Heck said, as Clint returned and put the beer down in front of the detective.

"What's that?" Clint asked.

"He's been looking for us."

"Have you got something?" Clint asked.

"I've got some connections for you," Polo said.

"Who?"

"You were right about the railroad guy, Parsons? He and Semple are on the boards of several companies together."

"A lot of people must be on those boards—"

"Semple owns a piece of the railroad."

"Ah."

"I also checked on the clubs he's a member of," Polo said.

"Semple?"

Polo nodded.

"Three clubs, and your man Frate is a member of all three."

"Again," Clint said, "that could be coincidence—"

"He was sponsored into all three clubs by Semple."

"There goes your coincidence," Heck said.

"Dominick, Heck and I have come up with a new theory," Clint said.

"Tell me about it."

Clint did the talking, explaining how they thought the entire thing might be an elaborate plan to kill Heck and make his death look like just one of many.

"What do you think of that?" Heck asked him. "Far-fetched, huh?"

"Not so far-fetched," Polo said. "Men with money—men who continue to *make* money—don't mind spending money to get what they want."

"So you think it's possible?" Heck asked.

"I think it's very possible. Want me to see if I can dig up a connection between the two of you?"

"Definitely," Heck said. "I'm impressed that you've come up with anything so quickly. See what you can find on me."

"Done." Polo drank half his beer and put the mug down. "I'd better get to it." He stood up.

"Don't you sleep?" Heck asked.

"Sometimes," Polo said, "but you're a detective, Heck. You know what it's like when you get on the scent of something."

"Yes, I do."

"Before you go, Dominick," Clint said. "Do you have Semple's address?"

"Sure." He took a piece of small notepaper and wrote it down.

"Why do you want that?" he asked, handing it to Clint.

"I just got an idea, and thought we'd work on it while you work on your end."

"If you find anything, let me know," Polo said. "We can compare notes."

"We'll do that. Thanks."

Polo left and Clint looked across the table and found Heck staring at him.

"You just thought of something, didn't you?" Heck asked. "Like two minutes ago?"

Clint nodded.

"The wife."

"Semple's wife?"

Clint nodded again.

"If he's stepping out with women like Deborah, what do you think she's doing?"

"One of two things," Heck said. "Either she's sitting home twiddling her thumbs, or she's stepping out on him."

"Either way," Clint said, "she's probably not very happy about him."

"You think she'd tell us something about him?" Heck asked.

"I think it's worth a try."

Heck took out his pocket watch and glanced at it.

"Tonight?" he asked.

"Ordinarily I'd say no," Clint said, "but since we know where her husband is . . ."

Heck pushed back his chair.

"You've got the address. Let's go."

FORTY-THREE

They grabbed a carriage outside the Alhambra and gave the driver the address of Aaron Semple's house. Clint didn't know what neighborhood they had ended up in, but the homes were huge, with big porches and white columns, almost as if they had been transported there from the South.

They went to the front door and knocked. When the door opened Clint wondered why Aaron Semple thought he had to go outside his home for his pleasure. If this was his wife she was lovely—on the other side of forty but still a very attractive woman.

"Can I help you? It's late."

"Mrs. Semple?"

"That's right."

"Ma'am, my name is Clint Adams," Clint said, "and this is Heck Thomas. We'd like to ask you some questions about . . . the Circle of Nine."

This surprised not only Heck but Clint himself, because he'd been about to say "your husband" when he abruptly changed his mind.

Oddly, it didn't seem to surprise Mrs. Semple at all.

"You're Heck Thomas?" she asked, looking at Heck.

"That's right, ma'am."

"I wondered how long it would take you to get to me," she said, folding her arms.

"Ma'am—Mrs. Semple," Clint said, "you've been expecting us?"

"Only if you were good," she said, "and I guess you were, because you're here, aren't you?"

"Yes, ma'am, we are."

"Then you might as well come in—and stop calling me ma'am!"

When Clint and Heck were in the living room, sitting on a sofa, a young man entered the room. Apparently, he had come down from upstairs.

"Virginia," he said tentatively, "is it—"

"It's not Aaron, Bill," she said, "but you should go. I have to talk to these men."

Clint realized that Mrs. Semple was dressed for bed and had thrown on a robe to answer the door. The young man's hair was tousled, and his shirt was out of his pants. Apparently, they'd been right about Mrs. Semple.

"But—"

"Go home, Bill," she said, pushing him toward the door. "I'll talk to you tomorrow."

Reluctantly, the young man left. Virginia Semple had the good grace to appear embarrassed.

"He's a sweet boy, but—"

"You don't have to explain anything to us, Mrs. Semple," Clint said.

"If I'm going to reveal my innermost secrets to you, Mr. Adams, you'll have to start calling me Virginia."

"Are you going to reveal something to us?"

"But of course," she said, sitting in an overstuffed armchair. "I swore I would, but only if you found me—and you have. A drink, gentlemen?"

"No, ma'am," Clint said, speaking for them both. "I

think we'd just rather have whatever it is you're going to tell us."

She sat back and arranged the folds of her robe just so before speaking.

"How much do you know about the Circle of Nine?"

"Not much," Clint said. "Only that they're hiring men to kill us."

"It was my husband's idea," she said, "but he needed a lot of other men to go into it with him, so he could hide behind them. Also, they'd foot some of the bills. He convinced eight businessmen—six here and two in Sacramento—that it would be profitable to them all if they were able to wipe out the last remnants of the Old West—the gunmen. Shootists, I think he even called you."

"But I'm not a shootist," Heck said.

"Of course you're not," she said. "You were the target."

"The target of what?"

"A revenge plot."

"Revenge for what? I don't even know your husband."

"He knows you," she said. "It's not surprising you don't remember him, Mr. Thomas, but he remembers you, very well. You see, my husband was not always the upstanding citizen he is today. At one time he was a common outlaw."

"How long ago?" Heck asked.

"Fourteen years. In fact, you put him in prison, Mr. Thomas."

"I did?"

"Yes," she said, "when his name was Jake Farmer."

Heck snapped his fingers.

"I remember Farmer. He had a gang that specialized in train robberies. I tracked them down and . . ."

"And killed all of them, except the leader. Him you sent to jail."

"He was supposed to be there for twenty years," Heck said. "Huntsville, in Texas, wasn't it?"

"He escaped after two," she said. "He changed his name, came here, and proceeded to become wealthy."

"He made all this money in twelve years?" Clint asked.

"Well, for one thing," Virginia said, "there's not all that much money. There's property, and there are businesses, but no money."

"But . . . he's playing in a high-stakes poker game right now."

"With the bank's money, no doubt," she said. "If you got to his bank tomorrow morning bright and early and made them check I'm sure they'd discover a shortage—one he means to return later in the day."

"Isn't he afraid someone will find out?"

"Like I said, you'd have to go down there and ask them to check. They won't do it on their own."

"Jake Farmer," Heck said, shaking his head. "Did you ever hear of him, Clint?"

"Can't say I have."

"They robbed seven trains before I caught them. Most of the money was never recovered."

"He used it to establish his identity here."

"Were you married to him—"

"No," she said, "I met and married him soon after he got to San Francisco. I thought he was . . . dashing."

"Why are you telling us all this, Mrs.— Virginia?" Clint asked.

"Because," she said, "I don't think he's dashing anymore."

FORTY-FOUR

Clint and Heck did present themselves at Aaron Semple's bank in the morning, along with a police detective introduced to them by Dominick Polo. They got the vice president to run a check and, sure enough, he found 200,000 dollars missing.

"He's finished," Clint said.

"And his Circle of Nine," Heck said, "eight of whom don't even know what's really going on."

"That doesn't matter," Police Detective Sam Kennealy said. "They're still in on the murders and attempted murders. What we'll need is for Mr. Semple to supply their names."

"Oh, I think he'll do that," Clint said. "I don't think he's going to go down alone."

"Clint," Heck said, "what if most of them are in that poker game?"

"What of it?" he asked. "They're not gunmen."

"Maybe not," Heck said, "but Jake Farmer was."

"But he doesn't have a gun. I searched everybody—oh, hell."

"What?"

"I'm getting senile in my old age," Clint said. "I searched everyone but Donald Frate!"

• • •

Frate came in and out of the room during the night to check and see if everything was all right, to see how the game was going. When he came in after nine o'clock he moved alongside of Aaron Semple and passed him a small .32 caliber, five-shot revolver while the banker was uninvolved in a hand and everyone else was.

"Your pot, Bat," the dealer said.

As Bat Masterson reached out to rake in his chips, Semple placed his hand on the table, with the gun, and said, "My deal."

The gun was pointed at Doc Holliday, across the table.

"Just sit easy, Doc," Semple said. "Bat, keep your hands on your chips."

Bat's hands were not only on the chips, but he was leaning forward awkwardly to get them.

"Don?" Semple said, and Frate produced a gun, as well, a normal-sized, six-shot Colt.

"Semple," one of the other men said, "not here. Not now!"

"Yes, now," Semple said. "I want to get this over with."

"But we're here, man!" another said.

"All of you gentlemen are part of the Circle?" Bat asked.

"That's correct," Semple said. "Seven of us here, and there are two in Sacramento who are missing out on the fun."

"What now?" Bat asked.

"Now we kill you."

"Just like that?" Bat asked.

"Just like that."

"And what about Clint and Heck?"

"They'll be taken care of," Semple said. "That's what the guards outside the door are for."

"And there are four of them now," Frate said.

"So we have a standoff," Doc said.

"What?" Semple said, laughing. "You call this a stand-off?"

"Considering I've got a gun pointed at your belly under the table," Doc Holliday said, "Yes, I think it is."

"You're bluffing," Semple said.

"Have I bluffed at all tonight?" Doc asked.

Semple's eyes flickered. It had been a long time since he'd been Jake Farmer, and the gun in his hand felt alien to him—but he had the drop on the man.

"Frate?"

Frate turned his gun on Bat.

"Even if you do have a gun," Semple said, "if you kill me, Frate will kill Bat."

"As soon as I pull this trigger, Semple," Doc said, "Bat will drop Frate."

Semple laughed shortly and said, "With what?"

Doc smiled.

"Make me pull this trigger and find out."

Clint and Heck entered the Alhambra and ran through the lobby to the stairs.

"Is something wrong?" Harold asked from the desk, but they didn't pause.

They were running down the hall and about to turn a corner when Clint put his hand on Heck's arm.

"The guards," Clint said. "If we're right, they're probably there for us."

"Right."

They both removed their guns from their holsters.

"Me first," Clint said. "I'll go low, you come around the corner high."

"Right."

"Ready?"

Heck nodded and Clint ducked around the corner and dropped into a crouch. Heck followed. . . .

When the shots came from the hallway it galvanized everyone in the room into action. Both Bat and Doc upended the table, dumping cards and chips all over the floor. Semple was pushed back in his chair, off balance, and as he tried desperately to bring his gun back to bear on Doc he saw Doc—empty-handed!—stand up and draw his gun.

That was the last thing he ever saw as Doc fired a bullet into his chest.

At the same time Bat flicked his wrist and a two-shot derringer appeared in his hand. Before a stunned Frate knew what was happening Bat fired both barrels.

At that moment the door was kicked open, and Clint and Heck came rushing in. When they saw that everything was under control they relaxed.

"You *were* bluffing," one of the men said to Doc from the floor. They had all thrown themselves down into prone positions to avoid flying lead.

"First time tonight," Doc said.

FORTY-FIVE

Detective Kennealy arrived at the hotel with some of his men in time to escort the remaining members of the "Circle of Nine" to the police station.

"What about the ones in Sacramento?" Heck asked.

"Oh, one of these men will give them up," Kennealy said. "We just have to put some pressure on them."

"I can help you with that," Heck said.

"You know their names?" Clint asked.

"I know one," Heck said. "Wesley Parsons, the president of the Pacific Coast Railroad. That's where his office is."

"So he hired you, just to set you up to be killed."

"It seems so."

The police also had to remove the six bodies—the four guards in the hall, as well as Semple/Farmer and Donald Frate from inside the room. Clint, Heck, Doc, and Bat decided to get out of the way so they went downstairs to the dining room for breakfast.

"Well, then, it's all over," Bat said. "Imagine that, it was all a plot to get revenge on Heck."

"A lot of people had to die," Doc said.

"And maybe more would have, if Semple's wife hadn't talked."

"Or Farmer," Clint said.

At that point Dominick Polo put in another appearance, presenting himself at their table.

"Guess what I found out?" he asked.

"That Aaron Semple's real name is Jake Farmer and Heck put him in jail fourteen years ago."

"Only he escaped after two," Heck said.

"And established himself in San Francisco with the money he and his gang stole from the railroads," Bat said.

Polo looked at Doc, who just shrugged.

"If you knew all this stuff why'd you hire me?" Polo complained.

"Join us for breakfast, Dominick," Clint said, "and we'll tell you how we found out."

After breakfast Heck went back to his own hotel to get some rest. He planned to leave San Francisco the next day.

Doc, coughing and looking worn-out, went upstairs to his room. He also said he'd be leaving the next morning.

Dominick Polo went back to his office to prepare his bill for Clint.

That left Clint and Bat standing in the lobby.

"Well, what are you going to do?" Bat asked. "Leave town also?"

"I don't think so, Bat," Clint said. "I like San Francisco. I haven't had much of a chance to gamble, and I've made a new friend. I think I'll stay awhile. What about you?"

"Another couple of days wouldn't hurt anything, I guess," Bat said. "Maybe I can get up a real high-stakes game."

"If you do I'll join you," Clint said, "but this time I'll search *everybody* for guns."

Watch for

WOMEN ON THE RUN

204th novel in the exciting GUNSMITH series
from Jove

Coming in January!

J. R. ROBERTS
THE GUNSMITH

JAKE LOGAN

TODAY'S HOTTEST ACTION WESTERN!

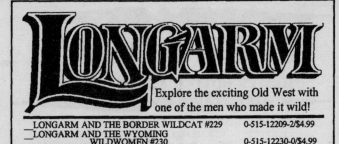